A Christmas Love Story

A
Zombie Survival School
Prelude Novel

WRITTEN
BY

Titus Strong

wunderlannd WP press™

MURFREESBORO, TN

1

Published by Wunderlannd Press
Wunderlannd Press Publishing LLC
Murfreesboro, TN 37130

A Christmas Love Story:
A Zombie Survival School Prelude Novel

To my mother, Nell Colleen Brown, who didn't want a horror novel dedicated to her. It's not a horror novel, Mom, it's a thriller with a bit of gore!

"I must not fear. Fear is the mind-killer. Fear is the little-death that brings total obliteration. I will face my fear. I will permit it to pass over me and through me. And when it has gone past I will turn the inner eye to see its path. Where the fear has gone there will be nothing. Only I will remain."

–FRANK HERBERT, DUNE
(DUNE CHRONICLES #1)

– Foreword –

By Titus Strong

I like surprises. In fact, I'm a sucker for them. This, my friends, is one of them. While attending a number of conventions over the years, I had a tendency to gravitate towards the work of comic artists and my love for comics and what they represented to me throughout my childhood.

You see, I grew up with comics in the household. My older brother collected comics and kept a stash in an old box that I rummaged through (without him knowing, of course) weekly, whetting my creative appetite with such titles as *The Savage Sword of Conan* (the black and white magazine version), *Conan The Barbarian*, *Judge Dredd*, as well as the fabled *Batman: The Killing Joke* and *The Dark Knight Returns*. Let's just say I was a normal kid with one fucked up taste in reading.

Nuclear Fallout, post-apocalyptic worlds, genetic mutation, all with a side of political satire and extra, hyper-gore violence couldn't stop me from reading each and every comic I could get my hands on. However, there were things in pop culture during that time, from movies to cartoons to comics that kept the heebie-jeebies and cold chills coming throughout my growth; and that, my readers, was...

... zombies.

From the cheesy ones on Scooby-Doo, where are you? to Michael Jackson's Thriller video, there was something to be said about these creatures that could take everything you loved and cherished and turn it into something so awful, so wretched, that you could easily replicate the classic horror movie scream and turn running away for a Panic Room to hide in.

But what scares us about them, folks? Is it just the fact that they are versions of us but in their natural progression of rotting? Is it the fact that they, too, desire brains just as we all do, looking for a way to fill our own brains with knowledge? Or is it the fact that they don't follow the norm of movie rules and come at you (and will) without hesitation, devoid of all motive but to feed, and will chew through every living thing to get to your soft flesh (hopefully while you're sleeping comfy in your bed) and not regret it one bit? It couldn't be that, could it?

Titus Strong
Zombie Enthusiast and Writer
July 12th, 2016
Murfreesboro, TN

A Christmas Love Story

A
Zombie Survival School
Prelude Novel

Written
By

Titus Strong

PROLOGUE

This is not something easy to say. In fact, it never is, especially when you have no one to say it to because they're all dead and/or have become The Dead. But here it goes anyway.

The world, as we knew, it is over.

The still figure stood on top of the double decker tour bus as it continued its route rather precariously through the snow-laden highway ahead, taking its time to allow the person hooked to the roof of the vehicle to do his job; to spot any incoming dangers ahead. This could easily be just a downed tree, meandering wildlife, or something wrong with the road itself. But what they mostly looked for, what the harnessed individual on the roof was known for searching out, was for The Dead.

*   *   *

The double-decker bus came to a halt not far from the city of Bloomington, Illinois, parking on the other side of a gas station. The road signs directing traffic into the city were covered with snow; in fact, everything was covered. The gas station was, the cars parked in the lot were, even the bodies that had been burned alive behind the great dumpsters just to the left of the station itself were covered, the Scout on top of the bus as well as the driver having only seen snow for the last few hours.

The troops slipped free from behind the

hydraulic set of reinforced doors and pointed their guns out into the freezing air, SWAT team style, moving to their designed places, their routines practiced almost in their sleep, quick and concise lines forming from their footfalls in the snow from their plodding forward.

Our plodding. We're plodders, that's what we do. Plod from one place to another, intent on finding something more than we did than the last time we stopped, Scout thought, keeping his own point secure on top of the bus by scanning the area around him with the night vision goggles on.

But the goggles wouldn't capture the heat from their bodies because there was none, Scout privy to this after watching a few of his own crew get eaten alive because of that simple mistake.

After the area was clear, they set up a perimeter, having the driver move the bus a little more forward to block the road completely, not allowing anyone to pass by them without having to get past the Big Red Bus, or BRB as everyone had been calling it.

Gordon, the driver of the metal monstrosity, had never told anyone the story of how he came to be in possession of the BRB, but everyone hoped that he would in the near future, maybe during one of their story times they held whenever they got the time.

In another moment, Gordon moved outside the BRB himself and closed the hydraulic doors with the remote key fob, watching as the doors hissed shut just behind him. He looked around, rubbed his gloved fingers and blew into them, looking up at Scout.

"Fuck nuggets, it's cold, Scout! I don't see how you stay up there so long on top of this beast! Most watchers can only stay up there an hour or so, but you just broke the three-hour mark five minutes ago!"

But Scout wasn't listening.   His eyes were staring intently at the fire that the others had just started, using an old metal drum as a cylinder to block the fire from the cold.   In another few minutes, the fire was blazing and they all crowded around the drum, hands exposed and out in the cold, grasping the warmth from the wisps of yellow and orange that flickered to life below them.

They had thoroughly sifted through the gas station and come back with bags full of food, items, and tools for the BRB to devour in its underbelly, two detailed to load it into the luggage bins underneath.   They hurried back after they were done.

Even Scout climbed down from his perch atop the BRB after scanning the wood line once more, using the small half-ladder that they had attached to the side of the bus for watchers.

"Whose turn is it this time," one of them asked

aloud, rubbing his hands together over the fire, shoving his gloves into his pocket the rest of the way so they wouldn't fall out.

"Derrick went last time," Gordon answered, motioning over at the thickly-bearded fellow across from him, the other man still bundled up to his neck in his cold-weather gear. He hadn't even taken his hands out from his pockets yet, his fingers still gloved as well.

"Damn straight I did," Derrick exclaimed through his beard, nodding over at the watcher next to Gordon who still stared into the fire.

"It's Scout's turn. He hasn't told a story yet."

Gordon looked over at Scout, who was the youngest of them all. He looked frozen to the core, frost still having collected on his newly-grown beard and on his eyebrows, his lips chapped and swollen.

I shouldn't have let him stay out as long as I did. He kept asking and asking to stay out until we all got here. That could have cost us a good watcher...and possibly the future.

Gordon interjected.

"No, he can go next time. He's been up on the BRB for the last few hours. Kid needs to warm up before-"

Scout answered for himself then.

"I'll go. I'll tell a story."

Gordon looked over at Scout, still somewhat concerned about the young man's welfare. After all, he was tasked to look after him until they got to where they needed to be. They were nearly there now and Gordon would feel awful if he didn't let to boy rest before they took the last leg of the trip into the city.

"Are you sure, Scout? You don't have to. I'm sure someone else has a story they can tell."

Scout looked over at the driver then, his eyes glistening in the flickering firelight.

He was going to tell them, Gordon surmised.

Gordon didn't know much about the boy; in fact, he knew the least of the boy's story than anyone that had been at the camp. But it was the cause that the boy told them about that Gordon followed now, which made him volunteer his BRB and all of his men.

Their livelihood was at stake, too. Their lives, their possible futures. It was worth looking at, this place that the boy spoke of.

The boy began.

"When my friend and I first came to your camp, we had already seen quite a bit. We're not just coming here to visit my old stomping ground. This is ground zero, where it all started."

The team around the fire shifted uneasily in their places, mumbling to themselves and others. They had heard this many times in the stories that were told around the fire. In the last few years since it had all started, the virus had wiped out entire countries all at once, in a stroke so clean that it had severed the ties to a world they no longer knew. Plenty of people had theories about where it started, several had even told stories about it, but none had bolstered the claim with truth.

"I know it's hard to believe, but it's the truth. It all started with a couple that were just going to a party. A Christmas party, with the whole spread of food and decorations, Christmas lights in the windows, with kids looking forward to Santa Claus coming on Christmas Eve. Hot chocolate and Christmas movies. Shopping at the mall, taking pictures with Santa; that's what this is about." Scout paused for a moment, letting the fire pop and crackle in the drum, looking from face to face before he began again. He looked at Gordon's face, into his eyes.

This will change everything, Scout thought to himself, but he knew it needed to be said.

"What I tell you now, well, I simply call it *A Christmas Love Story.*"

And it was then that Scout, the watcher tasked to the BRB and newest to the crew, began his story.

-1-

Thomas knew it for sure; he hated the fucking holidays. For the 28-year-old executive, not much made sense anymore. From the weekly outings for business that had long since began to tax his patience down to the finely-polished Stacey Adams dress shoes he wore, Thomas Gentry knew very little about his life anymore.

Driving on the snow-laden road up the hill to the Waterman Estate in the middle of the night was not his idea of fun. Yes, he had no problem with the free booze and his choice of lonely, liquor-induced secretaries and assistants during the holidays, but, with his arm piece of a girlfriend next to him in the car this time, he had little time for antics. In fact, Thomas had other things on his mind.

He had worked and slaved at Waterman and Associates for the last five years of his life, straight out of college and into a one-year internship, giving his time freely in hopes that there would be some pay it forward aspect in the near future. But, in the years working for George Waterman, he knew that he wasn't getting a partnership anytime soon. Those spots Waterman secured for only his most elite.

Thomas was never at odds with himself as much as he was at this moment. Driving through the thick blankets of snow that had come down for the last two hours, he and his girlfriend made their way as carefully as possible through the wintry weather to their appointed destination; The Waterman Christmas party.

All I can hope for at this point is an associate partner position, which is why I drove through all this fucking snow to get there on time.

A friend on the inside said that Waterman was rumored to be announcing the next associate partner position during his yearly speech.

An elaborate stance on the stairs leading up to his many-roomed mansion, some touching words to those that slaved away at his company while he took multiple vacations and fucked his third, hot trophy wife on his yacht, and a champagne toast at the end to consummate his success at other people's expense.

Yes, that was about it, Thomas thought, looking over at Nicole for the first time since they had gotten in the car together.

Nicole Simmons was born and bred for this type of life.

She was only with me because she thought I was going places in the company. Once she finds out I've gotten the position, she'll place herself strategically next to me for the win and things will be fine. I will have a sex-crazed nympho rich girl that has a trust fund from daddy that would make even the most well-off bachelor in Bloomington, Illinois do a double take at the prospects.

But, if I don't get the position- Thomas could kiss all that ass he was getting and the weekly blowjobs in the car at the drive-in from Nicole goodbye. She had simply been playing along in the game of life until the appointed moment.

And that appointed moment had come and gone last year, the young man agreed, knowing that this was his last chance at keeping her by his side.

He continued to drive through the snow, more intent than ever in getting a comfy position at Waterman and Associates.

*　　　　　*　　　　　*

"Welcome all to the party to end all parties!" George Waterman the Third lifted his glass high in the air, watching as the rest of his employees, family, and friends did the same. There were nearly one hundred people in attendance this year, though that number was still building every few minutes, due to the snow that fell outside his warm and inviting home.

"I'd like to thank you for coming to the Waterman family Christmas party and hope that you have a great upcoming New Years. It's not every day that we get to welcome new people to our close knit family business. There are so many new faces, much more than has ever been in the last few years." He looked over at his wife Claire, a woman fifteen years his junior, and smiled. She raised her glass as well.

It's your cue, honey, his eyes said, his dark brown eyes looking down at the crowd gathered at their feet, both of them with their three children at their side, a few steps up on the landing so they could see the sea of faces around them. Her eyes grew slightly wider with acknowledgement and she turned then to the crowd.

"And it is with our great pleasure to welcome you into our home on this holiday season to celebrate the 25th anniversary of our partnership with Stratford Square Mall and the many other companies that make Bloomington such a great place to live."

Not bad, George thought, *she might be a keeper.* He took a drink from his glass of champagne, letting that be the signal for all others to drink as well. They did, knowing it was the best champagne around, cases of it being shipped in for just this occasion.

And for the evening toast and declaration of

new positions for the coming year, George reminded himself, feeling for the index cards with his speech on them in the breast pocket of his Christmas tux. Once he felt them, he relaxed a little more.

Again, another point for Claire. She's falling into place nicely with the family and the company. He took another drink and finished the glass up, sitting it on the edge of the staircase as he spoke again.

"Eat, drink, and be merry, my friends!"

The live Christmas music was cued on time this year, the band dropping a sick beat before rolling into *Rocking Around the Christmas Tree,* the hustle and bustle around the staircase moving to places and parts all around the great mansion, the decoration lights coming on with the cue as well, all of the rooms lighting up like a great Christmas tree itself, George smiling to himself.

Again, done without a hitch or hindrance.

Looking like another profitable year for the company and for myself. He looked over to his wife, motioning to the rest of the crowd.

"Claire, dear. Can you find Mr. Phillips and see where my new hire is? I don't want him or his fiancée to miss the final toast of the night."

"Sure thing, dear." She smiled to the kids that were from previous marriages and elegantly, as practiced, made her way down the steps through the crowd, finding Mr. Phillips at the bar already.

"Mr. Phillips."

The portly, nearly-balding fifty-something accountant grabbed his drink and took a sip, turning to see his bosses' wife standing in front of him.

"Yes, Mrs. Waterman. How can I be of service to you tonight?"

"George is looking for the new associate partner he hired. He just wants to make sure everything is in place for his speech."

Just seeing the look in Mr. Phillip's eyes alleviated her stress. The old man's twinkle was just like Santa Claus in those old black and white films. His voice cancelled out all possibilities of failure.

"Say no more, Claire my dear! I am your man! I will notify the young man of the need for his immediate presence this instant!" He danced merrily away from the bar and away from Claire, bowing to her as he left, off to work his magic that only he knew how to work.

Claire breathed a sigh of relief.

Well, everything was going just as planned, as her husband said it would. Being a socialite is hard work, she admitted to herself, taking up a glass of champagne as it passed by on a serving tray, taking a long sip herself.

Now, just to wait.

2

"I'm just putting this out there; there's no other black motherfuckers like us going to be there!" Marcus exclaimed while driving, looking over at his soon-to-be other half as he watched the expression on her face.

He had known that taking the associate partner position would ostracize him from his own; from the darker skinned brothers that were struggling right now. But he also knew this was an opportunity of a lifetime.

He wasn't selling out; he knew that well enough. He was cashing in. Marcus Green had worked hard to get here, only now knowing that the "here" he had been looking for didn't have him surrounded by other darker skinned fellows.

The four years of going to college and missing out on the party scene at the frat houses and taking time to volunteer during his Christmas and Summer breaks in between semesters at school so he could get this job had finally paid off.

He was here; it was his time. And he was grateful to have his mocha-skinned Nubian queen Angela here by his side.

Marcus looked over at his fiancée of two years, who had stayed with him through thick and thin, and smiled. Somehow, in the smile that his fiancée Angela gave him back, he knew.

"But you knew that already, didn't you?"

She simply nodded her head and replied.

"It's about time then! We need to make our

appearance and make a good first impression. Hell, why do you think I bought a new dress? I don't mind hanging out with white folk!"

He should have known from that alone, looking at the cocktail dress on her now. Much of it was covered up with her formal winter coat, but he could still see the curves that the dress contoured as well as her fantastic legs.

He was glad that they had had sex first before leaving for the party; the sex calmed him and the orgasm kept him focused, which he would need to be, especially since the corporate party was more of a function for business than for pleasure.

And I can't let them think the new guy is a chump either, Marcus reminded himself, looking now out ahead at the snow that came down around them in sheets.

If we even get to make it to the party.

Angela looked over at him, seeing the nervousness on him.

"Are you sure you're alright to go tonight? We could always stay in and finish what we started."

Angela's proposition was a good one and warranted some serious thought on it, Marcus thought to himself, looking down at her freshly shaven legs, well-oiled and moisturized. But he knew that he couldn't. They already had a full schedule tonight.

"You know I wouldn't mind that in the least, but we need to be there. We're already running late. What is it with this fucking snow, man!"

And that just reminded him.

"Oh, babe, don't forget, we're supposed to be picking up Holden once he gets off work at the mall. I said we'd go see that new movie at the theaters."

Angela rolled her eyes jokingly.

"You two and your horror obsession. It's Christmas time! Who likes thinking about all that horrific stuff during the holidays? It's like mixing two completely different themes together, it just doesn't work. If anything, its tasteless."

"You're just saying that because you're scared." Marcus pretended that one of his hands was a spider, crawling up Angela's leg. She smacked it away.

"Stop, Marcus! You know how that shit scares me! The last movie we watched gave me nightmares for nearly a week!"

Marcus chuckled to himself.

"I'm sorry, baby. It's just a thing with guys and growing up. I was the same way when I was Holden's age. I loved stuff that scared me."

"Well, when you get home afterward, can we please watch something that has to do with Christmas, maybe a funny movie or something?"

She reached over and gave him a light kiss on the neck, the promise of something more, the guarantee that the night would be warmer than it usually was.

Marcus nodded his head slowly, letting her kiss on his neck a little more.

"I think we can fit that into our busy schedule."

*   *   *

Just a few miles away in a snow-laden building well hidden from civilians, Dr. Collin Moore buttoned up his lab coat, bypassing his winter coat in the coat closet completely, knowing it would bring more attention to him.

Almost there now. Just a few more steps and I'm free and clear.

The doctor felt the briefcase tap against his left leg, being sure to keep it tight against his side as he walked past security. They were busy with other things, the doctor having caused a spill in another wing of the building, watching as the distraction worked as perfectly as he had planned it to, giving them a quick smile as they rushed around the check-in/out area, Dr. Moore just another researcher walking past the contaminated area and out of the way so it could be cleaned, his eyes looking up at the cameras installed in the corners of each hallway, his eyes dropping back just as quickly so the monitors wouldn't think anything either.

Just a few more steps.

Ahead, he could see the emergency door. He knew that, after cutting the emergency door power earlier, the alarm shouldn't go off at all when he opened it.

If it does, I'm caught for sure.

He reached the door in a few more steps, placing his free hand on the door. He watched as three more scientists passed him by, moving to the secure area until the clean-up was complete, as per protocol. Dr. Moore pushed against the door and felt it give way, the cold air outside rushing in to meet him through the space between the door.

No alarm. It worked! Dr. Moore moved faster than he had ever moved, his feet crunching through the newly-made snow, the bitter cold hitting him with one great gust as he exited the top secret building, intent on getting as far away from there as possible. He tapped the button on the side of his watch, checking the timer.

Twenty seconds. I think I can make it in time.

19, 18, 17. The doctor crossed the empty parking walkway, walking into the dim light of the street light not far from him, then past to the remaining cars in the parking lot.

16, 15, 14. The cars were already blanketed with snow. Not just the hoods or tops of the car, but the entirety of the cars were covered, a few inches next to the tire even covered with the thick flakes that came down in hordes now.

13, 12, 11. The doctor pressed his key fob and heard his car start up a few cars away. This was the only way he could tell which was his car without drawing attention to himself any more than he already had.

10, 9, 8. He looked down at his watch.

Just a few seconds left. He lifted the briefcase by his side and popped both locks open, sitting it on the snow on top of the trunk.

7, 6, 5. He grabbed the thick glass vial with the milky green liquid that floated within it and shoved it into his lab coat, tossing the briefcase aside, watching it disappear into the snow.

4, 3, 2. Collin Moore then climbed into his car and pulled out of the hidden driveway.

"One." Just then, the power went out in the facility, sending the building and anyone in it into complete darkness. Dr. Moore had even been so clever as to disconnect the back-up power generator, so they would be left in the dark until someone figured it out.

Gives me ten, twenty minutes, tops to get free and clear of this place before they do a head count and realize I'm missing.

And that I have this. He pulled out the vial of *green liquid that formed and reformed itself inside the water, a cool-to-the-touch lava lamp filled with the future. Or our extinction.*

The doctor hadn't decided which one he was more interested in seeing. All he knew is that he had it now and that gave him the advantage for once.

They'll see. Oh, they'll see.

3

Wan had learned quite a bit in his twenty years as a security guard for the Stratford Square Mall in Bloomington, Illinois. First, the pay was shit. Second, he only stayed around for the medical and dental benefits.

And third, always have an unhealthy addiction that's portable. He smiled at that one, taking a puff off the Black and Mild, wine-flavored wood tip, feeling it fill his lungs with warmth, the cold

December air doing its best to bite through his pea coat.

He stood out on the roof now, looking out at the snow, at all of the Christmas shoppers that bustled in to get away from the cold outside. The parking lots were full, *more full than they ever had been before*, he took notice, looking over at the Century Theater and its parking lot, which had been filling up since there were no more spaces for shoppers in the regular lots now.

Down below, he heard a little kid complain to his mommy, stomping in the snow that he wasn't getting what he wanted as they walked through the snow to their car. Wan had an urge to roll up a good snow ball and chuck it at the kid, hitting him square in the head. But, whether it was his years of service to this mall or that he didn't give a shit anymore, the security guard couldn't tell.

I can't stand those fucking whiners, Wan thought to himself, taking another puff, watching as the plume of smoke drifted out and over the mall, floating over the hundreds of cars parked in the parking lot he had to police on the regular.

Right now, he was supposed to be in the mall security car, taking his second morning patrol. But he left it to one of the new guys. Wan didn't feel like going out again and again anymore. He didn't mind it once or twice a week, but there was no way that his aching bones would allow him to patrol four times a day.

I don't get paid enough to be Paul Blart. Wan tossed his half-finished cigarillo into the ash can near the doorway and made his way back into the mall, regretting it all the way.

Oh well, I guess it's time to make the doughnuts.

*   *   *

"Welcome to Yum-E-Buns, where you can try

our delicious buns for just $2.99 for a limited time through the holidays!" No matter how motivational or professional she said it, Melissa couldn't help but feel like she was demoralizing herself. And it didn't help when the senior crowd of morning patrons assisted with the jokey.

While the regular comments were 'I'll try some of your buns, honey' and 'I'd buy that for a dollar!' were their favorites, old Mr. Hughes broke the record today with a new one:

"Make sure they're covered with that warm white stuff before you serve them to me." His chuckle was not well meant; in fact, it was kind of creepy to the 18-year-old that had been working overtime at Yum-E-Buns ever since she graduated the previous May, with many of her fellow classmates.

Yum-E-Buns was a bonafide Cinn-a-bun and Auntie Anne's Pretzel store rip-off that had literally gotten popular overnight and, with that, began occupying many of the smaller town's malls that couldn't afford an Auntie Anne's or Cinn-a-buns.

All employees wore a bright blue visor that was printed with a white flag with the logo printed on it as well as the flag logo printed across an apron that they all were required to wear over their regular clothes, complete with a matching flag-shaped button that had their name printed cheaply on it. But the cashiers were lucky. They only had to wear the festive shirts for the holidays and the visor.

For Melissa, it didn't help that the Yum-E-Buns name printed on her shirt curved over her breasts, making them stand out even more than usual, the poor capital E in the middle nearly engulfed by the legal tender that were the fleshy portions of her body. The male senior citizens made sure to keep the logo in their sights as they counted out their change for their senior coffee purchase every morning after mall walking.

No wonder they took so long to count their change. I'm giving them a free show.

This was the highlight of her day; well, that and the moment she was told to go on break and took off to the roof to smoke with Wan, the security guard.

"I'll be sure to do that, Mr. Hughes." The only thing she could do was give him a droll response and not show that his comments were inappropriate and getting under her skin. He began to take the senior discount card out of his wallet but Melissa just waved it away.

"I already applied the discount, sir."

"Okay. Just didn't want you to forget, cutie pie." Old Mr. Hughes waddled away to the senior table with his change in hand, half a cup of coffee and a handful of creamer packets in his grubby paws.

Melissa messed with the snake bites on her bottom lip, turning them over and over in her fingers, a nervous tick that she had gotten since getting them a few months back. Her hand went nervously to the nose ring on her left nostril that had a small band aid over it until she got off work, looking out into the crowd of shoppers as they passed by. Melissa looked back in the back of the store and tapped on the counter.

"Somebody needs to take him off his Viagra medication. He's a public menace." Melissa could hear her friend Will chuckle through the prep center in the back, working on the order that had just popped up on his screen.

"Just get used to it, Mel. You're a pretty girl and the manager sticks you on the register for that **very reason. You** sell yummy buns!"

He passed her the cinnamon buns with extra icing for Mr. Hughes, sliding them down the warmer tray, then clicked the order off the screen in the back room.

"Ha, ha. Very funny, Will. Why don't you try selling Yum-E-Buns to little old ladies? Or better yet, some of our thick sausages rolled in Yum-E-Cakes. I'm sure they'd love your juicy, black sausage between their buns!"

Will's chuckle diminished just as quickly as it had come and the true understanding of sexual innuendo blanketed over him, his face contorting at the thought. He may be black and he may be a perverted teen that thought of sex all the time, but he drew the line at gilfs.

"That's just wrong, Mel."

"Equal rights, equal wrongs, that's what I always say, Will. Enjoy the image. I'm going to deliver my buns to this old man and hope that he doesn't die of a heart attack." She placed the buns on a tray and delivered her best sexy starlet pose with a departing kiss onto her hand at Will, sauntering out onto the patron floor and into the wandering gazes of half a dozen senior citizens.

How could this day possible get any worse?

4

Holden McCall slipped his backpack over his shoulder, doing his best to perfect his wavy, brown hair in the mirror before tucking it neatly into the Yum-E-Bun visor, rushing out the door of the group home to the shuttle van going into town. He saw the van pull up just as he shut the door behind him.

"What took so long, Mr. Martin?" The thirty-something pudgy group counselor with graying temples just shrugged his shoulders at the teen as he put the van in gear and pulled away with a number of teens in the back. Holden got shotgun since he was the oldest of them all.

"You know how it is, Holden, adult stuff: A lot of paperwork and gathering the rest of the kids going to meet Santa before the holiday rush gets there."

Holden sat his bag on the floor in between his legs in the passenger seat, looking back at the masses of kids going to the mall with Mr. Martin.

"Well, I'm sorry to be the bearer of bad news, but the holidays are in full swing there, that's why they called me in today. They say it's going to be the busiest it's been this whole year today, with the field trips, Christmas shopping, and holiday events starting today."

Holden suddenly began to dread accepting the shift added to his never-ending shifts ever since he graduated high school months earlier.

But then again, there was Melissa. He had

checked her schedule when it was first posted this week and saw that she worked today.

It's finally happening.

He was going to do it today. Holden was going to ask her out.

However, for Holden McCall, she was vastly out of his league, had a good family, and was prepping for college in the spring; she was too good to be true. She would be leaving out of town shortly after Christmas, just a little over two weeks away, so the love-struck teen didn't have much time left to tell her how he felt. He just hoped she felt the same way.

And I hope Wan is on break on the roof so I don't have to walk all the way around through the front entrance to clock in. Holden was sure that he would be late if he had use the front entrance.

Yes, everything was falling into place for Holden McCall. He had a decent job that he didn't hate to the core, he was moving out of the group home after the New Year, and he was going to ask out the girl of his dreams today before she left work.   Life was certainly shaping up to be something more than it started out for him.

What could possibly go wrong?

5

The snow came down in the thick blankets now, the sun setting in the western tree line not far from the hidden drive that Dr. Moore had left behind only minutes earlier, hoping beyond hope that he would make it out of Bloomington before it got too dark. Once out of town, no one from the facility would know where he had gone.

When they sent the authorities to my residence in the city because of what I had stolen from them, they'd find nothing.

He had left no clue as to where he was going.

He had not text it, emailed it, or written it anywhere for them to find. Unless they were mind readers, Collin Moore was a free man.

He flipped on his bright lights and peered through the haze of snow, watching as his wipers did little to assuage the problem.

It was the amount of snow coming down, it practically blinded him from seeing any further than the front of the hood.

Well, at least it will hinder those that will come after me as well. And I have a good 20-minute head start. He smiled at the thought of them trying their best to look for him, questioning everyone he had talked to within the last week or month.

He felt the weight of the vial in his pocket, wanting to drag itself down onto the seat the rest of the way. But he kept it close to his leg, making sure it didn't get out of his reach.

Years of research, so much of my time put into

something so small, so powerful.

He knew what they had planned to do as well. He had seen the documents that they were planning on sending. He was surprised he was able to access their databases so easily.

They were going to ask for my resignation or discredit my research and bar me from the facility once this was done.

But the joke was on them. I finished it early.

Collin laughed to himself at the thought of duping an entire military research facility. That's why Dr. Moore didn't see the deer standing in the middle of the road through the snow, his car slamming into it at full speed. The front wheels lost their grip on the road for a second, just long enough to send the car careening off the road and into the woods several feet below.

Collin Moore slammed into the dashboard and that was all he remembered.

*   *   *

"Can you even see outside this windshield, Marcus?" Angela did her best to squint her eyes and look for the road ahead, but it was no use.

"Yeah, I can see. I see the road just ahead. It's veering to the right now, see?" Marcus followed the road right, watching as the last of the sun set into the tree line just ahead of them.

"Well, shit! That doesn't help a bit. Without the sun, there's only so much I can see with the headlights. Here, let me try them on bright." He switched them onto bright but he could barely see out in front of the hood.

"Baby, I think we should go back. It's getting too dangerous. They'll understand. I mean, look at this. It's a White Christmas before Christmas!"

But Marcus was hard-headed. Angela already knew what the answer was going to be before he said it.

"Naw, baby. Let's just drive a little slower, I'll be careful. Only a few more miles and we'll be there." He looked down at his GPS, which showed the route only being minutes away.

"Marcus, look out!" Marcus looked up in time to see a deer lying on the road, his car sliding a little on the snow as his wheel finally caught traction and slowed them down. The deer was lying out on the road in front of their car, the headlights showcasing the gore of its mangled body.

"Holy shit, that was close!"

"I already told you not to be looking down at that phone!"

"I got it, I got it!" Marcus looked out at the deer, who was still moving just a little bit, it's blood turning the white snow underneath into a crimson slushie.

Marcus couldn't exactly go around it. It was in the middle of the road, blocking both lanes of traffic. He was going to have to get out, he knew.

"I'll be right back." He moved to get out but Angela stopped him.

"What exactly do you plan to do, Marcus?"

"We can't exactly drive over the deer! I'll move it out of the way, onto the side of the road, and we'll drive around it and keep going."

Angela had a moment of fear pass over her face but then Marcus grabbed her by the hand.

"I'll be right back."

Marcus opened the car door and watched as the blankets of snow fell on him, covering his winter coat in moments. He slipped on his winter gloves and walked over to the deer, standing in front of the idling car.

It was a buck, and a big one. It laid on its right side, eyes frozen in fear, staring out into the woods. Its front two legs were broken and bones were protruding from the skin, a slash on his stomach sending his intestines spilling out onto the snow under him. The intestines steamed in the cold air and the great buck snorted and tried its best to shift itself out of the threshold of pain, still staring out into the woods.

Marcus walked around him and reached for his back legs, grabbing up the thick paws in his hands. The buck jumped out of surprise but didn't try to escape; it looked too weak to escape.

Marcus began dragging the buck off the road, to the left side, when he noticed it. There was a fresh clearing in the trees not far from them. And, as he looked down on the road, he saw the faint trail of tire tracks that veered off to the left, straight down into the clearing. He dropped the buck's legs and walked over further to the edge.

And, not far from the edge of the road, he saw more. It was a car. And it was still running, or still giving off heat, he noticed, a steady rise of steam from the smashed-in engine.

He pulled the buck into the bushes and ran back to the car, wiping his hands in the snow on the ground right as he got there.

"There's a car that's wrecked in the woods down in the ravine! I think that's the one that hit the deer."

*   *   *

"What happened?" Dr. Moore shifted in the driver's seat but then felt a sharp pain in his ribs, making it difficult for him to breathe. He felt the pressure in his forehead and realized then that he most likely had a concussion.

Just relax, Collin. Everything will be fine. This is a busy road. Somebody will pass by and find my car on the side of the road in the ditch.

He didn't know how long he had been out, but he did notice that the sun had already set and the car and himself were blanketed in darkness and snow. He tried looking through the cracked windshield for any signs of where he might be on the road or if he could even get out, but it was already covered with snow and more was falling.

Then he heard a voice.

"Hello? Hello, is there anyone in there?"

Dr. Moore stuck his hand out of the broken driver's window and waved it despite the pain in his side, letting them know he was there.

See, that wasn't so bad! Dr. Moore unbuckled his seat belt and waited for the cavalry.

6

"Will you look at these motherfuckers right here! Just clearly owning the parking lot on this muggy December morning!" Wan lifted the wine-flavored Black and Mild to his lips and took a puff, watching as the three teenagers below in the parking lot laid waste to the security car with a flurry of snow balls as it patrolled its daily perimeter, a frightened newbie behind the wheel.

My fault for that, Wan accepted wryly, staring down at the security car from the rooftop that he used for his own personal break area, the kids far from done. This was his second break of the day and much needed.

Apparently, these kids had spent some quality time making hundreds of snowballs by a parked car in the parking lot adjacent to the main road that circled the mall.

From up here, it looked like they had military training, the old man thought, trying his best to hide his salt and pepper hair under his knit security beanie.

But it was no use. He was nearing fifty early next year and he just had to except it; he was an old codger now. He was the old man the kids snickered at when they passed, he was easily the most perverted old man in the crowd, far from being finished from getting ass but too old to find it easily.

Just five more years and I can hit early retirement and walk around this place without being in uniform.

The thought of this made him smile, taking another puff from the wooden tip, letting the smoke surround him as he watched the winter war below, it finally taking a turn for the security guard he had hired two weeks earlier.

A van Wan knew all too well stopped not far from the security vehicle below, the Yum-E-Bun employee Holden hopping out of the group home van, his gloves on, his backpack thrown over his shoulder. He grabbed up some snow from the sidewalk and ran next to the security car, tossing a heavily-packed snowball at the three teens.

The snowball exploded across the side of their cover car, rolling down and around them all. This prompted the security guard to put on his flashing lights and climb out once in park, doing the same. In another moment, the odds had been somewhat evened, the newbie security guard taking notes from Holden and fighting back, double snow balls tossed up and over the car, one exploding across the cover car while the second wild snowball impacted across one of the teen's faces, nearly knocking him down.

"Well, I'll be! Looks like we got some game down there now, by golly!" The old, black man straightened his security belt and put a foot up on the ledge to watch the festivities below when he spied Holden staring up at him from behind the security car. Wan simply nodded and reached down, pressing his door release key fob hanging from his belt to let Holden in through the service entrance.

The door four floors below buzzed and stayed unlocked for 20 seconds, which gave Holden a small window to get there, the young man ducking for cover as he rushed for the door, dodging the random snowballs as best he could. If anything, it gave the newbie security guard a chance to get a few well-placed shots in on the teens before he got back in his car and moved along, back on his route, the world as right as rain as far as Wan was concerned.

Holden nodded back up at the lead security guard as he disappeared inside, Wan finishing the last of his cigar before making his way back into the chaos of the holiday mall season.

"You have the right idea, young blood. I guess it's time to get back to work and stop dilly-dallying. Here I come, motherfuckers!"

Wan put out the cigarillo on the ledge in front of him and straightened up his belt, pulling his security beanie down over the edge of his ears, feeling the cold wind breaking through his dark pea coat, pulling the collar up around his neck as he turned to go inside. He dropped the cigarillo into the makeshift ash tray next to the door and walked back into the warmth of the mall.

It was beginning to get dark already. The sun was going down over the hills just to the west of

Stratford Square Mall in Bloomington, Illinois and this old man knew that, when it got dark, things got crazy at the two-story mall.

All the little mall freaks come out at night, wanting to start some shit. Well, I got something for them.

Wan patted the thick, black Maglite at his side, feeling the weight of it in his hands as he unholstered it and spun it around a few times, clicking it on to go down the rooftop hallway.

*   *   *

Little Tommy Seaver loved Christmas. He had never seen anything like it in all of his six short years alive. Out of all of the holidays throughout the year, Christmas made him the happiest.

His mother took him by the hand and showed him all the wonderful things around him during Christmas time. That was there special thing together.

In fact, Tommy still remembered the last two years of doing this with his mother, her bright smile and beautiful smelling hair one of his favorite things about her. He looked at the others in front of the two of them and at the long line that nearly wrapped around the great Christmas Tree that stood, brightly-lit, poised behind Santa Claus himself. It was difficult for Tommy to contain his excitement this year, for he had spent a great deal of time making a special gift for Santa.

His mommy had told her little boy that Santa didn't get presents like other people did. Instead, he was always fulfilling the wishes of others and never thinking of himself. And, yes, she confirmed that the milk and cookies were just as source of energy that Santa Claus needed to get from place to place in such a hurry.

'A trip like that around the world burns quite a bit of calories for one person, wouldn't you think,' his mother had said weeks earlier while unloading the groceries.

But something didn't settle right in little Tommy Seaver's mind about the most giving person in the world not receiving a gift himself during such a festive season.

So the little boy took to his room with crayons, markers, and blank construction paper, creating the most colorful hand-made holiday card a six-year-old could make, spending hours after hours thinking about meeting Santa and finally giving him the gift Tommy Seaver was sure that he always wanted.

*   *   *

Cornelius Prescott looked through semi-blurred vision at the line that formed and wrapped around the giant Christmas Tree and stretched down and across the south side of the mall, a collection of

Christmas-goers, screaming children, and impatient parents and family that waited with bated breath for the man in red.

He was now the one they looked to for comfort during the dreary and death-laden holiday season. Cornelius's clothing was that of Christmas fantasy: his thick physique had been adorned with the red felt coat with furry collar and cuffs, his slacks were now the same matching color, complete with a fuzzy red belt with a brass buckle. He smiled when he thought of where he first saw Santa himself, when he had just been a mere child.

It was here at this very mall, the old man remarked to himself, thinking now that it had been nearly 55 years since that moment that had changed his life forever.

But that had been when it was just an outlet, before the big companies had even built their cornerstones that trumped the rest of the rather small mall on each end.

Sitting in his 61-year-old body now, he still had trouble wrapping his head around the concept of becoming what he had always loved since he was growing up; Santa Claus.

But time had taken its toll, Santa agreed, nodding his head as the next child was sent to him by the photographer in front of him, Cornelius blinking several times to get a clearer view of the world around him.

The world was beginning to spin. He could feel the dabs of sweat begin to form under his arms and up his back, Santa shifting once to let the undershirt dab at the sweat. He would take his lunch break in an hour or so then he would change his under clothing entirely. Sometimes his undershirt and underwear were soaked through after wearing such a thick suit.

It didn't breathe, the material. And I like to breathe. Remind myself to not take two pills next time. Too much. Way too much.

The little boy sat on his lap and smiled up at him, two front teeth missing from his smile. But somehow that didn't matter to Cornelius, a.k.a. Santa Claus, who hefted the child as if he were a rag doll, plopping him properly onto one knee as he gave his best jolly old laugh that he had in years.

"Ho, ho, ho! Merry Christmas, little boy! And what is your name?"

The little boy simply handed Santa his list. The day continued on as planned.

7

Holden slipped the festive Yum-E-Bun smock over his head and tied it quickly behind his back. One of the motion activated buttons on the smock went off as he finished tying it.

"Welcome to Yum-E-Buns. Here, try our tasty buns," the digitally recorded voice of Bun-E, the Cinnamon Bun mascot said, almost too loud for Holden to think.

Yes, the piece of flare was up to its former hijinks today, Holden reminded himself, hoping and praying that the button didn't do what his previous button had done before its demise, which was nearly run out of battery power and get stuck saying, "Our tasty buns, our tasty buns, our tasty buns," over and over again until Holden went on the roof during his break and took a hammer to it, ending its short, mocking life as a button gone wrong.

Will was in the back, working a double shift as always. Open to close, that's how he liked it, get the shifts out of the way and have three days off in a row.

Holden had no idea how Will could persevere as he did, Holden barely about to take 6 hours of a shift at the cinnamon bun shop, let alone 12 hours, with prepping and closing combined.

And there was Melissa. She was put on the register, as always when Herb was here. He said it brought in customers, which it seemed to do, the eighteen-year-old looking out at the lobby at the full crowd that watched as Melissa policed the floor, picking up trays and cleaning off tables periodically to keep the place clean. Her mid-length blond hair was tied back so it didn't touch her collar and she had the Christmas Yum-E-Bun shirt on as well, the tight fit accentuating her curves in all the right places, enough to drive a teenager mad with lust.

Well, at least drive me mad, Holden thought, clocking in a few minutes late on the computer screen, *but nothing that would get me in trouble with Herb. After all, the guy was a softie when it came down to it.*

He understood Holden's situation, being in a group home, and what his commute encompassed, knowing that it would never be the boy's fault for being late in the first place.

Behind him in the break room/stock room, Holden could hear his manager rummaging around in the Christmas decorations.

"Anybody see Bun-E's head? I know I left it here

with the rest of his body two days ago."

Will passed by and called out to him.

"Herb, someone left it on the top shelf to air out yesterday. They sprayed it down with disinfectant after they were done and wanted to keep it away from any food or product."

Will pointed up to the top shelf where, indeed, the bulbous head of the cinnamon bun mascot lay.

"Well, shit! Previous day's shift needs to start leaving a note when they do anything out of the ordinary. I spent 15 minutes digging through all these boxes thinking we had lost the head. Not on my watch! Not on my shift!"

Everyone on shift with Herb knew that Yum-E-Buns was his life's blood, that each and every day he strived to make it better and better for the customer, forever spending his life pleasing complete strangers over coffee and some pre-made frozen cinnamon rolls.

God, please don't curse me with his purpose, Holden reminded himself, pleading with the big man upstairs, *let this just be a pit stop to something greater.* He smiled over at Melissa as she passed back through the counter area, putting up the spray bottle and cleaning rag back under the counter.

"Well, look who it is, if it isn't Holden McCall, December's employee of the month!" Melissa mockingly stood over against the wall in her best Vanna White pose, showcasing the cheesy picture of Holden that Herb had taken last week in the sliding plastic sleeve. It sat above December...and November...and October. Holden had been employee of the month for the last three months running, much to the chagrin of everyone else that worked there.

"Alright, I get it, Melissa. It's high time that someone else get a try. I completely agree." He kept himself humble, allowing her to be her silly self and smile her beautiful smile at him. He allowed oh so much to be done to him just to be near her. If she asked to punch him, he would lean his face out so she could get a good shot.

But he was not without come backs, one of which he delivered at that very moment.

"Well, when someone finally gets as good as I am, I guess they can have the spot. Who knows, with all the New Year's resolutions being made, maybe one can strive to reach perfection here like myself." He pretended to breathe on and shine up his fingernails, watching as her mouth opened in awe at his blatant big headedness.

"Well, if Holden isn't in rare form today, Will!" She punched him lightly in the arm and he liked it oh so much.

"Yep, that's Holden alright. Full of himself as ever. What's the word, turd?" Will smiled at Holden from behind the cook's area.

"The word is I got off for New Years!" Holden

waited for the two of them to spazz out, which they completely did. While Melissa flapped her arms in protest, her mouth still open in even more awe, Will pretended to shoot himself with a gun finger over and over again, making pretend bloody messes all over the back room. Melissa was the first to speak.

"New Year's Eve! How did you spring that? This is ridiculous! I asked off for that like three weeks ago!" Will raised his hand in unison.

"It was five weeks ago for me, broheem. How'd you snag it? The schedule for the next two weeks isn't even out yet."

He looked at them slyly.

"Employee of the month for three months straight has its perks."

Herb countered, sitting Bun-E's fuzzy mascot head on the counter.

"Yes, indeed, it does, Holden. Which includes first shift in the suit. Take your late ass on the rounds with a tray of the expired buns."

"Ooooh, snap! You heard the man, get your buns to work!" Melissa exclaimed, covering her mouth jokingly. She smacked Holden on the ass as he passed by her, his head down in mock defeat, carrying the mascot head to the stockroom so he could change.

8

"Hey, mister! Try and stay awake. You might have brain damage." Marcus looked quickly back to the man that they had found on the side of the road, keeping his eyes peeled for the driveway of the Waterman Estate, *which should pop up at any moment, based on the GPS that was navigating them through the snow storm.*

The doctor held his head, lying back on the backseat, a blanket Marcus had in the trunk used as a makeshift pillow.

"It's Collin. Collin Moore."

Angela looked down at the man's lab coat questioningly.

"You a doctor, Mr. Moore?"

"A scientist."

"We're you on your way to the party?"

The scientist slipped the badge off his lab coat and handed it to Marcus.

"What party?"

Angela looked over at Marcus. "Guess that answers that question."

Marcus continued driving, slipping the badge into the pocket in his slacks. He was focused on driving more than ever now.

"Wait, I think we're here! Doctor Moore, we're going to get you help!"

*   *   *

"He said they were on their way. They should be here any minute, Mr. Waterman." But Mr. Phillips could see that George was not amused. There were three wrinkles that his boss got on his forehead when he was highly agitated. At present, Mr. Waterman had two of the three wrinkles.

Just then, there was a knock on the door.

Mr. Phillips' face brightened with the alcohol contained in it.

"Ah, there they are now!" He moved over to the door and opened it, a bit surprised at what he saw on the other side.

It was Marcus and Angela Green; however, Marcus was carrying a still figure in his arms that was covered up in a blanket.

"Is there a doctor in the house?"

*   *   *

"Where did you say you found him again?" Indeed, there was a doctor in the house. Several of them, to be correct. But Dr. Ibsen Charles raised his hand first, moving to the wounded man's aid.

In no time, Mr. Waterman had a room opened up for them and Marcus and the doctor took him up the stairs to the spare bedroom, lying the man down.

"I found him in his car. He didn't say anything except for his name and that he was a scientist. I think he was too weak from the accident."

The doctor inspected the man's head, using the tips of his fingers to feel the scalp.

"Probably a concussion. It happens with most forward motion injuries. Just a bit of trauma that suspends the ability to use cognitive protocols. He should be fine if there's no internal bleeding. I've got this, son. You did a good thing, saving this man. He could have died there in the cold without medical attention."

Marcus hesitated to go. He didn't feel like a hero and didn't want what came with the title. But he felt tied to this stranger for some reason, as if the man were his responsibility now.

"I hear from George that you're the man of the hour. Go accept that associate partner title in front of the hundreds and call it a day. After a few handshakes and a few cocktails, you can always come back up here then make your way home whenever you like." The new associate partner nodded in agreement and made his way out of the room.

Marcus shut the door behind him and made his way downstairs, straightening up his bow tie. His suit hadn't gotten bloody but his winter coat had, which he took off now, folding it in half so the dried blood didn't show. He saw Mr. Waterman coming up the great stairwell to meet him halfway.

"What a way to make an entrance, Superman!" George clapped him on the back, walking down the stairs with him. Marcus could see Angela near the main entrance way and he nodded to her. She smiled and gave him a thumbs up, grabbing a drink from a waiter's tray as it passed by, taking a long drink from the glass.

"So, are you ready for the introduction?" Mr. Waterman looked down at his new associate partner's bloody winter coat and shook his head disapprovingly.

"I'm sorry. Let me get that for you." George lifted his hand in the air and a waiter was there within seconds, looking to Mr. Waterman for his appointed task.

"Yes, Mr. Waterman?"

"Can you take this garment and have it cleaned in the laundry room and pressed within the hour?" The waiter nodded his approval and took the coat. Marcus stopped him short for a second.

"Wait, I need to get my things out of it!" Marcus grabbed his keys, some note cards, a pack of gum, and a small wrapped gift the size of a jewelry box, stuffing them into his pockets.

"Thank you, Mr. Waterman."

"Not a problem, Marcus.   And its George." George grabbed a drink from a nearby tray and handed it to Marcus.

"Have a drink. It'll take the edge off after an ordeal like that."

They walked and mingled through the crowd for a bit, side by side, just letting the scene of so many people take their attention from all that had just happened. Then Mr. Waterman stopped and looked quizzically at Marcus.

"I saw that he was wearing a lab coat. Is he a doctor of some kind? I don't know of any hospitals in this area."

*   *   *

Collin Moore had slipped in and out of

consciousness throughout the drive with the couple, but he was wide awake in the plush bedroom when he died in front of the unknown doctor.

At first, the pain was excruciating. It was like a flow of water the size of Niagara Falls trying to fit itself inside of a garden hose, the pressure inside of Collin making his body seize up in pain.

"Calm down, doctor! Collin, is it? That's what Marcus said your name was from looking at your doctor's badge. Collin, I need you to focus on my voice. My name Dr. Charles and you've been in an accident."

But Collin focused instead on his own heartbeat, which grew more faint with every beat. He could feel something stronger than his heart pulse inside of him now. The longer he listened, the better he knew where to decipher where it came from.

"My leg. My leg, it hurts." Collin managed to sit

his head up a little, looking down at his lab coat.

"Your leg, you say? Let me see." Dr. Charles looked down at his leg, noting that the pants were coated in dried blood. The doctor went to move Collin's lab coat when he heard broken glass and noted that the lab coat was stuck to the pants as well. Dr. Charles managed a peek inside the lab coat pocket and took out the broken vial that Collin had put in there. Dr. Moore looked down and saw shards of glass sticking into his own leg, the contents of the vial nowhere to be found.

Dr. Charles continued. "Now, the only thing I can do for that wound is stabilize it for the moment. We'll need to get you to hospital and get those shards removed and stitches."

But Collin just shook his head. He could feel what was in the vial flowing through him now. It burned every cell it touched, turning his insides against him. He grabbed for the doctor.

"You've got to get out of here! You and

whoever else is here. It's too late!"

But Dr. Charles just chuckled lightly and began tying a makeshift tourniquet on Collin's leg.

"Listen, you'll be fine. After a few stitches and an X-ray, we'll have you good as new."

And that's when Dr. Collin Moore felt his heart stop beating completely and his body fell back onto the bed. Doctor Charles hadn't even finished tying the makeshift tourniquet on him yet.

"Oh my god! Collin! Doctor! Can you hear me?"

Doctor Charles leaned in over the other doctor, listening for a heartbeat. Finding none, he checked the poor man's pulse, waiting a few moments before giving up the search entirely. He began C.P.R., pressing down on his chest and giving mouth-to-mouth resuscitation to the recently deceased.

*   *   *

The waves of a new sea within Doctor Collin Moore arose within him then, crashing against the previous version of himself, the weaker version, tearing apart all the limits that had been set inside of his psyche, that had been placed upon his frail form since its inception.   Deep inside, the unknown substance found its strength, found a new home within its host, transforming a dingy, hollow world inside into an intricate layer of nerves and synapses, triggering and firing anew.

*   *   *

In another few moments, Collin's eyes flickered open. Doctor Charles breathed a sigh of relief.

"Oh, for heaven sakes!   Thank goodness!   I thought I lost you there for a second!" He patted Collin on his shoulder and felt the other man shudder in response.

"It'll be okay, my friend, we'll— " The rest of the words stuck in his throat as Collin lunged at the poor doctor's jugular, tearing his teeth into new flesh; fresh, warm blood and pulsing arteries that refused to stop flowing until the entire body was void of fluids. The dead Dr. Moore saw to it that Dr. Charles was nothing more than a void. He began tearing at his flesh, ignoring the gurgling protests completely.

9

Thomas Gentry was three sheets to the wind. He had spent the last hour liquoring himself up until he could get the courage to go talk to Mr. Phillips and ask him what he had wanted to ask him for nearly a year.

Who got the associate partner position? It was me, right? It has to be me.

But this was all in his head. He could see Mr. Phillips entertaining a few others just a few steps away but Thomas trouble moving to get there. He took his first step.

Then his second, then third. Soon, he was standing right next to Mr. Phillips, listening to a pseudo interesting conversation about stock options and the old, fat man's last trip to Tahiti.

Thomas tapped Mr. Phillips on the shoulder. The older man turned, a liquored smile on his face.

"Well, if it isn't Mr. Gentry, gracing us with his presence! I was wondering when you were going to come by and say hello. And I see you've brought your lovely lady, what's her name again?" Mr. Phillips looked around for Mr. Gentry's other half at the party but didn't see her.

"Nicole. It's Nicole. And yes, it's very serious. But I don't want to talk about that." Thomas pulled Mr. Phillips aside, whispering in his ear.

"Who got associate partner? That's all I want to know. Let's just call it an early Christmas present to me."

Mr. Phillips' entire face seemed to sober up then. He may be old, but he wasn't a walking mat.

He yanked his arm away from Mr. Gentry, taking care to keep his voice down.

"You're drunk, Thomas. While I have no problem with that, I really think you should evaluate what you say to others before they take it personal."

"I've worked my ass off at this place, Phillips!" Thomas didn't attach the Mister title on purpose, wanting to get a rise out of the old man. And it did. Mr. Phillips was about to speak when Mrs. Waterman passed by, grabbing Mr. Phillips by the arm lightly.

"My, what an interesting conversation that's going on right in the middle of the party. How about this, Mr. Phillips; George says that he needs you because he's about to do his speech now and I'll take Mr. Gentry to the bar and let him get some coffee to sober up before his drive home."

Mr. Phillips concurred and scurried off to Mr. Waterman's side, Claire wrapping her arm underneath Thomas's own, holding him up to keep him steady.

"You didn't get the position and you're making yourself look like a jackass in front of everyone. Come with me."

*   *   *

"Ladies and gentlemen, I apologize for the delay but, as you saw, we had an emergency. It is all well taken care of. I have my best doctor taking care of the poor man and he's said to recover just fine." Mr. Waterman reached out for a glass of champagne and took a fresh one up into the air. He held it there, taking a few steps up onto the staircase.

It was toast time.

"I'm sure you all have had some wine and food prepared by the caterers, but you are all probably waiting to hear the real news, who will be filling the new associate partner position for next year. Well, I have the person here now and would like to introduce him."

*   *   *

The Dead Collin Moore licked his fingers clean of the blood from the still form of Doctor Charles' carcass, lifting himself up from the floor. He moved on all fours, listening to the hum of voices beyond the half-closed door.

He could hear the pulses of each person downstairs, some faster than others, some slower. His body shuddered again at the thought of so many tastes all at once, so many to choose from. He crept down the hall, following the sound of the voices.

*   *   *

"It was a long and arduous task of finding someone to help lead this company but, after a long interview process, I think it's best to say that we've found our perfect match." Mr. Waterman motioned to Mr. Marcus Green, the man of the hour.

Marcus had never smelled flesh before. And we're not just talking the superficial layer of flesh, either. The scientist, Doctor Collin Moore, moved across the balcony stairway so quick that it was difficult to see who it was at first. It wasn't until that he was teeth-deep into Mr. Waterman, tearing into the side of his throat, that Marcus took notice.

KERRRRIIIPPP! Blood gushed out in rather healthy spurts and there was a quick, pained gurgle as Mr. Waterman flailed about, losing his footing on the stairs as he reached for the wound instinctively, bringing back a hand covered in bright, red blood and bits of torn flesh, still wide-eyed that he had not yet finished his speech.

His body fell forward but the person behind him was sure to buffer his fall. The raving scientist tackled him and they both slid down the bloody steps towards the rest of the guests, the scientists gaping maw pulling Mr. Waterman closer and closer until-

A nearby woman let out a blood-curdling scream and the world around Marcus was suddenly thrown into chaos.

It wasn't like in the movies where someone valiant came forward and defeated the monster standing in front of them. Many were cowards, most were just smart, moving for the exit at once, not bothering to look for their coats, which had their keys and personal belongings in them. It was a sad day for humanity.

By the time Mr. Waterman's body had stopped convulsing in shock, the scientist had already fed on three more of the crowd, the bodies lying in puddles of red at the foot of the stairs.

Yet, Mrs. George Waterman was nowhere to be found.

10

"Oh, fuck yes!" Claire Waterman steadied herself against the sink as Thomas rammed his cock into her from behind, taking all of his frustration out on not getting the associate partner position on the wife of the one to blame.

"You like that, don't you, Mrs. Waterman? When little Thomas takes care of you like this?" Claire simply nodded her head in approval and grunted, keeping her dress high enough so he could continue his work.

Thomas felt empty inside. All of his work for some foothold to climb the corporate ladder here was gone, with no hopes of him ever becoming anything in this small fucking city.

Bloomington can suck my dick, Thomas thought to himself, grabbing up a handful of Claire's hair in his free hand, looking back over his shoulder once to see if anyone's shadow was near the bathroom door. There was a flurry of movement outside the bathroom but no one was listening in on the little quickie that he and Mr. Waterman's wife was having.

Thomas felt her climax on his rigid member and he continued on himself until her moans and gyrations brought him to orgasm as well, slowing his pace as he let go of her hair, placing his hands on the arch of her well-tanned hips to steady himself.

Claire's wispy voice came from over her

shoulder, a slight layer of perspiration across her brow glinting in the dim bathroom night light.

"Well, that was exactly what I needed, Mr. Gentry."

Thomas pulled his slacks up from around his ankles and adjusted his boxers, buckling his belt back the way it had been before he had heard the awful news outside.

I can't fucking believe it! And the position was given to some new guy again! This is ridiculous!

Claire had finished adjusting her dress back the way it had been and was dabbing at her eyeliner with a piece of tissue. She looked over at Thomas in the mirror as she was running her fingers through her hair to get the tangles out when she took note of his sour face.

"Well, I've seen better faces made after I've fucked somebody like that, I can tell you that much!"

Thomas smiled through the anger. "It's not

that. Your ass, tits, and pussy were amazing, Claire. It's just that I was looking forward to getting that position."

She turned and smiled at him then, patting him on the chest. She could feel the perspiration through his dress shirt. The shirt clung to his skin a little bit more than it normally would, something that Claire had known to look for time and again with her husband after he had been at work with his "meetings" late into the night. That's why she didn't feel the slightest twinge of guilt when taking Mr. Gentry up on his lascivious glance earlier.

"Maybe I can do something to help that along a little, Thomas. After all, I do have some say at the corporate level, be it that I own 35% of the company."

Thomas' eyes widened with interest.

"Really, you could do that?"

Claire had finished straightening her hair at the bathroom mirror and moved for the door.

"I can do anything. The question is, what are you willing to do for me?" She gave him a look and a wink, the seasoned sex pot reaching for the door.

"We can work out all the details later. But, for now, let's get back to this boorish party my husband is having. I'll go out first. You wait two minutes and then go out after. I'll be sure to say something to George tonight before the party is over. Sound good?"

Thomas couldn't imagine anything sounding any better. He couldn't wait to get out that door and back to the world so he could celebrate properly.

With a rum a coke, and maybe a few more after that. Fuck it, I'm getting wasted. Nicole can drive us back through the fucking snow tonight.

Claire opened the door then and the commotion outside in the main foyer leading to the stairs was almost deafening. She had no idea why she hadn't heard it before when she was in the bathroom with Thomas.

Oh, that's right, I was being fucked properly. And the fan was on.

She never got to laugh at her perverted thought because a blur of movement in front of her sent her flying back into the bathroom, hitting the floor at Thomas' feet.

"What the fuck!" Thomas reached down to pick her up. She didn't seem hurt from the fall, just shaken up a bit. That's when he saw the blur of movement again, this time it moved into the doorway.

Dirty, disheveled, and covered in blood, Mr. Phillips moved for Claire quicker than Thomas had ever seen him move.

"What the hell happened to you, Mr. Phillips?" But Mr. Phillips was lost in thought, grabbing for Claire's ankles to drag her closer. That's when he took a bite of her. Both Claire and Thomas screamed out loud.

"Oh my god! What the fuck are you doing, Mr. Phillips? Stop!" But the old man didn't hear or didn't care about Mr. Gentry's pleading cry. Claire lifted herself up from the floor and tried to fight Mr. Phillips off of her, but his rather thick self blanketed over Claire almost perfectly, grabbing for her hair to hold her still.

Thomas lurched forward to push Mr. Phillips away but felt an arm swing back at him in retaliation, the old man throwing him back into the wall with such force that the dry wall cracked behind him.

Thomas looked outside the half-open door for help but found none, nothing but shouts from a distance and quick flurries of movement that he couldn't quite see clearly enough to tell who they were. He looked for something to attack Mr. Phillips with and quickly decided for the back of the toilet basin, swinging it wide to use momentum to get the wild Mr. Phillips off of Mrs. Waterman.

"Ugh!" The basin made full contact and cracked his old corporate buddies' head open, dropping him to the floor in a heap just next to Claire. The basin broke into several pieces and Thomas dropped what was left of it in his hands onto the floor.

*   *   *

Marcus grabbed for the door and bolted out of the back door past the caterers, Angela's hand tightly in his own.

Angela was nearly in hysterics when she spoke. "Did you see that? Did you see that, Marcus?"

Marcus nodded his head and pulled the car keys out of his pocket, hitting the unlock button on the key fob. Already, the snow had created a thick layer over each car, making them all look the same.

He hit the unlock button again, looking for the white lights to show through the snow.

Nothing. Fuck, I didn't want to have to do this. He looked back behind them. Still, no one had tried to make it out through the back doors where all the cars were parked.

It was too much chaos at the moment. People were just trying to get away. He pressed the alarm button and the valet area lit up with sound and red lights, the red lights shining through the snow just enough so he could see which car was his. He and Angela ran to it.

But others ran as well. Their movements were quick and fluid, almost as if they were feral animals, the infected of the party dropping down on all fours to claw through the snow to get closer to Marcus and Angela.

"Marcus, they're coming!" Angela had no quicker said it than saw four infected approach at such a pace that it was hard to comprehend.

"In the car, quick!" Marcus cracked his door open enough to slide into the driver's seat, shutting it quickly behind him and locking it. Angela did the same, one of the infected attendees slamming into the door at near break neck speed. It slid off the door and into the snow just behind the car.

"Get your seatbelt on, Angela!" Marcus revved the engine and hit the wipers, letting the snow fall away from the windshield enough to see the other three infected guests bounding towards them.

Marcus hit the gas and they took off down the snow-covered street. But so did the infected.

11

"Are you okay?" Thomas looked down at Claire, who was presently nursing her wounded leg. She winced in pain as she lifted herself up with the help of Thomas, leaning against the sink they had previously fucked on.

"No, that motherfucker Mr. Phillips was trying to eat me!" She looked down at the still form of Mr. Phillips, his skull caved in, leaking out brain matter on the nice tile floor that she had gotten redone after the last wife left.

"What the fuck is going on out there? Are they

doing flakka? I heard about that drug and what it does. Mr. Phillips was tripping when he came in here!" Claire tore part of her dress and used it to tie around her wound, Thomas suddenly sobering up more than he ever could with a cup of coffee.

"What do we do? I mean, there could be more of them out there."

But Claire wasn't deterred, not in the least. From high-functioning Christmas parties, fucking on the spur in the bathroom, to dealing with drug-induced employees, she was one cool chic.

Thomas could see why Mr. Waterman had picked her as his present trophy wife; she was cool under pressure.

"My husband has a gun collection downstairs in his study behind a bookcase. I think if we make it there, we'll be a bit safer. Unless you want to keep using porcelain toilet pieces as weapons." She nodded down to the broken pieces all over the floor. Thomas shook his head.

"Lead the way, Claire. I shall follow."

Claire took three steps toward the door and stopped. She seemed to be listening for something. Thomas could still hear a number of screams outside in the main area and saw movement outside the doorway, but nothing came in after them after Mr. Phillips.

Thomas whispered out to her.

"What is it, Claire? Do you hear something?"

She turned slowly around, her head twitching slightly to one side, her hands shaking as well.

"Thomas, I think-" The explanation never came out. Instead, the bite she had acquired on her leg began to itch, her entire body on fire on the inside, her eyes glazing over with some unknown filter that showed her a world she had never seen before. And there was an intense hunger.

Claire felt it start in the pit of her stomach and then branch out to all of her limbs, her brain the most acutely aware of all her organs, honing in on the beating, pulsing organs of Thomas Gentry. Claire bent down for a quick second and bounded onto Thomas Gentry, knocking him to the ground, the shards of the porcelain toilet piercing his back. He cried out but that only intensified Claire's frenzy upon him, her fingers digging into his skin.

Mrs. Waterman fed like she had never fed before.

*   *   *

Marcus and Angela felt the tires slipping and sliding down the hill but they both felt better off traversing through the icy conditions than meeting the problem head on that they had just been witness to.

"Did you see that? That doctor just ate your boss! He just took a chunk right out of him!"

Marcus nodded his head. He could feel the lump of fear in his throat rising and it felt as though he could vomit just by opening his mouth; so he stayed silent, instead focusing on the winding road ahead of them, which was covered with snow and was icing over now.

Angela looked over at her fiancée. His face was covered in a light sheen of sweat and the whites of his eyes were large and nearly bulging out, trying to focus on the road conditions in front of him.

"Marcus, are you alright, baby?"

Marcus felt his body convulse and he slowed the car down so he could open the door and vomit, his stomach tied up in knots, the nausea coming in waves. The car came to a halt halfway down the hill, Marcus letting all of the nervousness and tension out on the side of the road, simply leaning out over the snow-covered street was enough for him. The fear, anxiousness, and turmoil he felt all came out in the snow, his stomach slowing its churn until it stopped completely. In another second, he was back up, wiping his mouth of the spittle that had formed at the side.

Not far up the hill, he could still hear screams echoing from the mansion. He even heard another car start its engine.

Another car could be down this hill any minute. This narrow road doesn't leave much room for two cars side by side, especially with the snow coming down.

"I'm better now." He shut the door and lurched the car back into drive, moving at a quicker pace than before.

"Where do we go, Marcus? The police?"

"Did you see how fast that doctor turned those others? It was almost instantaneous once he bit into them. We have to go get Holden and warn the rest of the city. Most of them will be at the mall. This road leads right into the middle of town and the mall is at the center of it. If those infected make it down the hill, this city is gone for good! They'll have no chance!"

Angela nodded in agreement. She looked at the dotting landscape of the city just below them. They could see the lights from the mall and the surrounding buildings from the road they drove on now. It was always a picturesque view when being so high up. Everyone came up to this hill to get a more scenic view of the city during the fall and winter seasons. The local photographer even took postcard photos from this vantage point.

It was hard to imagine that this place had just been so full of carnage and death, Angela thought to herself, looking back at the road to the mansion they had come from, their tire tracks nearly covered up now from the heavy snow falling.

They continued on.

12

Thomas Gentry and the other guests of the Waterman Christmas party lifted themselves up from their places on the floor. The pulsing inside them told them to do this, moving them outside into the snow-covered landscape not far from the mansion. There were small scatterings of echoed screams nearby, but their hunger called for more than just a few bites on another party guest. Down below, looking off from the great hill that the estate had been built upon, was Bloomington,

Illinois.

The mall was at its center, filled with bright lights, the bustling of the Christmas time shopping almost able to be heard from such a distance away.

None of The Dead took the main road down. Instead of following the winding, snaking trail all the way down, they ran straight down the hill, skipping past all the safety that had ensnared them formerly, throwing all caution to the wind, their bodies launched down the snow. They tumbled and fell and felt the freedom from restraint for the first time, their legs pumping down the hill, pushing them to limits that they had never felt before. Some broke limbs, shattering spleens, impaling themselves on branches and sharp rocks during the tumble, but they continued on nonetheless.

The damage to themselves mattered no more. Only the feeding mattered. In a few minutes, they had cleared the majority of the hill, the ground leveling out to the streets of the city, the great, two-story mall shining up before them. The Dead continued on.

*   *   *

Thomas Gentry had always hated malls. They had never been his favorite places to go to; the hustle and bustle, watching his ladies try on outfits for hours at a time. Even when he was younger, around 10 or so, his mother would drag him shopping on the big sale days, taking him out for lunch at his choice of fast food afterward.

It was fast food and the arcades in the mall that he enjoyed the most. However, as his alert form shifted and bounded across the snow, the mall offered up so much more than it had when he was a youth. Outside, the lights nearly exploded in his eyes, capturing his attention more than they ever had before.

Dead Thomas could see within the automatic glass doors thousands of multi-colored lights, some blinking, some not. And the movement within the building; it was exquisite. It was as if a pool of warmth and light generated from the mall as a whole, each individual within it giving off their own energy.

Thomas felt himself drawn to this place, felt himself drawn inside, the doors sliding easily open for him, closing behind him. Once the doors closed, he could hear the music ringing in his ears, the conversations being had, though they were just murmurs to him now; life pulsed through this entire place, his mouth salivating at the thought of it.

But everything changed when he saw a thick red form not far from him, surrounded by other warm masses, his nose picking up the smell of warm meat just a few feet away.

He called out to see if anyone would answer him.

*   *   *

Cornelius Prescott lifted himself up from the chair, hearing the grunts from the far away onlooker as he came rather close rather fast. He bypassed the line completely and bee lined it straight for Santa. Santa Claus motioned to security and they moved just as quickly.

"Security, we've got another one!" Cornelius pointed at the man moving towards him, so much surety in his steps that he thought the person knew him from his outside life of being Santa Claus. But, as the man closed in, Cornelius knew immediately what type of person it was; some homeless vagrant, smelling like something dead. It was easy to decipher this once the smell his Cornelius' nostrils.

The smell almost knocked him down. He waved the stench away but realized then that security was just a moment too late. The homeless man was on Cornelius in an instant, biting and tearing, trying to rip at the Santa Claus suit Cornelius wore, the man's fingers cold to the touch.

"Whoa there, buddy!" Cornelius strong-armed the homeless guy, keeping him at an arm's distance until security could get ahold of him.

His skin was clammy, too, Cornelius noticed, pushing the man as far away as he could, security grabbing him by the arms as they led him away from the photo area. That's when Cornelius remembered that there was a line of parents and children just behind him, having watched the entire thing.

He turned to look at all that had just seen the entire thing. And there, at the front of the line, was the cutest little boy with his mom. Santa waved his hands out to all the little boys and girls in line that were frightened or stirred up by the occurrence.

"It's alright, ladies and gentlemen, boys and girls. Just a little misunderstanding during the holiday season. My little mall helpers have handled the situation and Santa is back on track with his regular schedule of pictures with the kiddos and free peppermint candy!"

Cornelius said the last part with some motivation, listening as the kids and parents shouted with glee, the same jovial spirit the crowd had been in coming back rather easily.

Security really should get a better hold of the mall, especially during Christmas time. They know how crazy things can get.

Santa sat down in his great chair and ushered the next child forward.

*   *   *

Wan listened to the static on the radio as the downstairs Santa security team went wild. He squeezed the call button and answered back.

"You're saying there's some crazy guy that tried to attack Santa down there with you **now**?"

The rattled new guy's voice broke through the static. "Roger that, Wan. He just came out of nowhere and bum rushed Santa."

Wan was concerned. He took a sip of his coffee from the Yum-E-Buns on the second level, looking down at the commotion that had been caused by the attack.

"Well, is he okay?" It took a moment for the newbie to report back.

"Who, Santa?"

Holy fucking shit! Who are hiring these kids? They can barely tie their own shoes nowadays!

"No, the Easter Bunny! Yes, Santa Claus! Is Cornelius okay?"

"Yeah, we got to him in time. He's back at his chair. He seemed to calm the crowd down a bit."

Wan looked over at the employees at the Yum-E-Bun. By now, they had heard the news from the walkie and were all staring at Wan to see what he would do. The walkie broke static again.

"So, Wan, what do you want us to do with this guy? We got him restrained at the moment, but this guy is out of it, probably high or something."

It starts. Always around this season, the crazies come out to ruin every normal person's good time. Christmas time, at least to Wan, was a time to forget about all the short comings and failures of the previous year and prepare for the new year by being grateful for what you have, spending time with family.

Homeless people always gotta be fucking with people's happiness!

"Hold'em in the conference room until I get down there. I'll be down in the next 10 minutes."

"Copy that." The static broke and was silent again.

For this situation, I'm gonna need to have a smoke first.

Wan motioned over to the crew at the Yum-E-Bun, nodding his head to them before he began to walk up to his spot on the roof for a quick smoke.

"Looks like Christmas is coming early for Mr. Security Guard, guys. We got a homeless biter down in the lobby."

Melissa wrinkled her nose at the thought.

"Ew, gross!" She finished wiping down the tables in the store and waved bye to Wan. Holden moved away from the cash register and came over to her side, helping her throw away some trash from a nearby table.

If there was ever a moment, it was now, before she got off work. This was her last go around on the tables before she left.

"Hey, Melissa." The gorgeous co-worker of his dreams turned with a smile.

It was now or never.

*   *   *

Little Tommy Seaver could see Santa Claus now, up close. He was next in line and he even made eye contact with Santa, the jolly old elf smiling back at him as he sat down in his great chair, grabbing a candy cane from his red bag next to him.

That's where the toys come from, too! How does he have room in that bag to carry so much, let alone all the toys for the girls and boys of the world?

Tommy Seaver's mind was racing with possible answers. His hands were getting sweaty, his mom noticed, drying them off with a tissue that came from out of nowhere.

"It's going to be okay, Tommy. He's been waiting to see you, too. You know the song, remember?"

In less than the span of a second, his mind recalled the song his mom was talking about. He nodded his head.

'He sees you when you're sleeping, he knows when you're awake, he knows if you've been bad or good, so be good for goodness sake.'

Tommy lived those words as his mantra for the last year, making sure that he was being good, that the word 'bad' didn't come out of his mom or dad's mouth once. He lived to please everyone around him just so he could get here, at this one spot, with a clean slate to show Santa how good he's been this year.

This was his chance to make his dreams come true. Tommy smiled at the thought of all of his dreams coming to pass then, knowing it would be the bestest Christmas ever.

13

Cornelius lifted the thick Santa cuff to one side, noting that the random guy had bitten his hand but not penetrated through his tough gloves at all. But his forearm, that was another matter altogether. Beneath the fluffy, white cuff, there were teeth marks that had broken through the skin, leaving little red dots of blood where teeth had broken through the superficial layer of skin.

It didn't hurt at all. For Cornelius though, *it itched like a son of a bitch*! And, underneath the surface of his pink, fleshy skin tone, something with a green tint swam around. It wasn't just within the veins, though it did go there as well, but ran across his forearm in a web-like pattern, moving up his arm. And it burned like nothing Cornelius had ever felt before.

It was as if his eyes were awash in a transparent layer of something had glazed them over. His head swam for a moment and he released the cuff of his shirt, grabbing for the arm of his Santa chair to steady himself. The photographer noticed Santa stumble a bit and went to steady him but Cornelius simply waved her away.

"Just got up too fast, that's all. I'll be fine." But Santa wasn't fine. He was better than fine. Fine couldn't describe the feelings that he was having throughout his entire body.

The glaze over my eyes was simply a filter of sorts, Cornelius deduced, being able to pick apart the pieces of the world around him his eyes had never been able to do.

The colors were amazing to him now. The décor of the entire mall blew up like fireworks to his eyes, the yellows exploding like the sun, the blues erupting like the skyline in a cloudless afternoon.

But the reds; the reds were something else entirely. Just the Christmas tree bulbs on the tree behind Santa pulsed with a new life, Cornelius looking around at the crowd and then out at the rest of the mall as it pulsed with a life he could only see.

"It's beautiful," he told the photographer, ushering her back to her station, Cornelius taking another quick look before sitting back down in his chair, the tips of his fingers tingling with a newfound sense inside the gloves.

And in front of him, next in line, was little Tommy Seaver, holding his picture he had drawn Santa as a gift; a gift he had worked long and hard on. Cornelius' eyes had trouble veering away from the colors on the picture, staring at the reds and yellows, the blues, and the greens that the child had painted just for him.

"Go on up there, Tommy. Give it to Santa." His mother ushered him up onto Santa's lap and Tommy did as he was told, hopping up onto Santa's lap, staring at the old man quite intensely as he offered him his gift.

"I got this for you, Santa. I thought you could take it with you when you delivered your presents to the other girls and boys."

Santa Claus smiled. It felt good to smile. It felt good to move any and every limb, *almost as if it were controlled by some greater force than his own*, Cornelius thought, reaching out for the gift the little boy had made for him.

"Tommy, is it?"

"Yes, Santa."

"Well, I thank you so much for this gift, Tommy.

It's not every day that I get-" The little boy interrupted him, pointing at his face suddenly.

"Gee, Santa, what's wrong with your face? Your eyes are bleeding." Cornelius could feel little Tommy beginning to scoot down off of his lap in fear, so Santa let the picture drop to the ground as he grabbed for the boy with both hands, bringing him closer.

They're bleeding now so that I can see it! So that I can finally see!

Cornelius looked closer at the little boy, at his skin, at the layers beneath, as his eyes that showed the pulsing, beating veins beneath, pulsing so loudly that it sounded like a freight train passing Cornelius by. The sound was horrific and felt as though it went on forever, Cornelius opening his mouth to scream. But the scream stuck in his throat.

He felt a warmth then flood over his mouth and lips, down his beard, continuing to flow until the train passed, his eyes glazing over even more now.

Instead of the freight train in his ears, there were screams coming from all directions. His eyesight focused in on Tommy's mother's face, contorted in pain and horror. Cornelius went to reach out and comfort her when he suddenly felt the weight in his hands.

The little boy, Tommy had been his name, was still in Santa's firm grip, a pale white image of his former jovial self. His left arm was torn in half, the flap of flesh and bone spurting out blood all over the floor in front of the Santa chair on the Christmas Tree printed rug in front of all the other parents and children.

And, in Cornelius' other hand, was the half-eaten forearm of the little boy, still tender and plump in all the right places. Santa Claus smiled at the thought of this and took another bite.

*   *   *

"I was wondering, when I get off later tonight, would you like to go to the movies?"

Melissa blushed. "What, you mean, like a date?"

Holden felt the lump in his throat, felt it swell and take hold of his tongue, not letting him speak. He could projectile vomit now but could not get the words out. He fought past his fears.

"Yeah, kinda exactly like that. I like you, Melissa. I've liked you for a- "

Melissa and Holden heard the screams and the scattering of people below near the middle of the mall, their attention diverted for the moment. Down below on the first level of the mall, they watched as security darted towards the line to see Santa.

Holden heard Will move from behind the cook prep area and took off his visor.

"Holy shit! What's happening, Holden?"

Holden just shook his head, the crowd full of parents and children running from the Santa display, a security guard not far away hitting the floor with a thud. He lay at the edge of the tree line within sight for another moment and then was pulled into the Santa display, out of sight.

Melissa covered her mouth, speaking in hushed tones.

"Oh my god! What's happening? Are we being attacked or something? Is this a terrorist attack?" The only answer was a scream and crunch and then all was silent save the screams of the departing crowds.

And then they saw him. Santa Claus moved away from the tree line, his eyes a yellowish-green, his white beard covered in red, spatters of dark red all over his outfit.

Will's eyes grew wide. "Is that Cornelius; like is that Santa Claus- eating somebody?"

He stared at the chunk of bloody mess that was

in Santa's hand and watched in another second as Santa chewed on it, tearing sinew, muscle, until there was a piece ripped from it in his mouth. He sucked it down his throat, flecks of blood flying into the air.

And there were others besides him; others that moved and crept differently than a normal person. They moved about and lunged at others, climbing, biting, ripping, tearing, until that normal person fell to the ground and was still. After a few bites, the person was no longer still. They got up, too, and began the same routine as the others.

Holden didn't intend on watching anymore to see what happened. He had enough visual stored up in his head for a lifetime already.

"To the roof! It's break time! Wan will know what to do." Melissa and Will didn't hesitate and followed Holden through the inventory receiving door of Yum-E-Buns and left the rest of the mall behind.

*   *   *

Wan sat atop his mall perch, smoke in hand,
trying to figure out what to do with that damn
homeless man downstairs in the conference room,
when he saw a crowd bust through the doors
below, looking back once before running to their
cars.

"What the hell is this? Has everybody lost their
minds tonight?" He took a puff off his Black and
Mild and watched the scene play out.

But the shoppers never made it to their cars.
They were accosted by things on all fours on both
sides, leaping and springing towards them in the
snow. Powdered snow sprang up in all directions,
families screaming as they were attacked in the
parking lot, blood staining the white snow on the
ground.

Wan grabbed his walkie and mashed the

button down hard.

"Ryan, this is Wan! Contact the local police! We got some gang activity or something going on down on the East side of the mall!"

He let go of the button and waited for a response. No static, no nothing. He was about to try again when he took notice of the movement below. And that a few of them were looking at him.

They had heard the walkie talkie. They looked up at him and he knew then that it was no gang activity, no violent protest or uprising going on. What he saw on their faces showed him that.

The creatures were people, well-dressed, too, but much of what they wore was either stained or ripped beyond recognition. Their bare, bitten flesh showed in the moonlight. They growled at him with a mouthful of flesh and bone.

And then they began climbing up the wall.

"Holy fuck! Oh, sweet Jesus!" Wan turned to

run as fast as his legs would carry him when he nearly ran into the three from Yum-E-Buns.

"Mother of God, do you guys not know how to warn somebody you're there?" Wan could feel his heart racing, his eyes on the ledge of the mall, his Black and Mild on the snow, having fallen out of his mouth. He shoved the walkie in its holster at his hip and began backing away.

"Alright, kids. Back stockrooms only. We're going to take the scenic route. Those things are coming up the walls!"

He reached down for his keys and unhooked them from his belt, looking for the all-access card that opened the doors just down the stairway.

"We can stay back there for days until all of this blows over. There's stocked up food for all the food court in the freezers in the back." He slipped his flashlight out of its hook on his belt and clicked on the light.

"But it's pretty dark down there."

Melissa screamed as one of The Dead landed on top of Wan, slamming him down into the snow so hard that he dropped his keys and flashlight.

"Umph!" The impact had knocked all of the breath out of the security guard so, when he tried to get away, he was gasping for air. The three stood riveted in fear as more climbed up the ledge, moving for them as well.

"What do we do, Holden?" Melissa looked to him then to Will, who both were still trying to grasp all that was going on.

Wan cried out on the ground as The Dead tore into him, its eyes filled with excitement at finally getting a taste through the thick pea coat, spitting out the chunks that it didn't want onto the ground.

It took everything that Holden had to move. There were other Dead almost upon them and he knew that they would be victims in another moment. Holden reached down for the set of keys and the flashlight, turning the flashlight around to its base. The Maglite was heavy in his hands as he swung it, making contact with the Dead on top of poor old Wan.

Blood sprayed out of its shattered jaw and across the snow, the creature flailing backwards onto his back. Holden didn't wait to see if he had killed it.

"Come on, Will!" He grabbed Melissa's hand and rushed the three of them through the rooftop door, shutting it behind them. Holden locked it with the heavy bolt and slid the all access card across the reader until it turned green, sealing the door shut. They heard The Dead slam into the door on the other side, scratching and clawing to get at them. They could also hear Wan's cries for help. After a few more screams, the old security guard grew quiet.

"He's dead, Holden! He's dead and we let him die!" Melissa muffled a sob and Will covered his mouth in panic-stricken horror. Holden just sat in the darkness for a moment, trying to gather his wits about him. The young man could feel the lump in his throat harden and he fought back the overwhelming sadness pulling him into the darkest places of his mind. He gripped the Maglite as hard as he could in his hand and turned it on, leading them down through the stairwell.

"Come on, guys. We need to keep moving."

14

Marcus and Angela never made it to the mall in time. Driving through the mall parking lot, they could see that now. Bodies lay scattered across the snow, the Dead moving from carcass to carcass, chewing on what they could until something else caught their attention.

"We're too late, Marcus. They got down here before us."

Marcus could feel the tears well up in his eyes.

"I just hope that Holden made it out okay. He's a resourceful kid. He knows where we live. We need to get there and barricade ourselves in until the military comes. That's all I know to do. It's not safe on the road."

They drove off, their headlights turned off as they moved away from the parking lot to keep the creatures away.

*　　　　　*　　　　　*

Holden used Wan's access card and got into places that none of them had ever seen. First, they walked through the back stockrooms of all the mall stores, boxes upon boxes stacked up for the holidays, some of the more expensive items in metal cages locked up tight.

"I bet there's a key on these set of keys that opens all those cages, guys." Holden lifted up

Wan's keys. But suddenly he was filled with guilt at not trying to save Wan until it was too late.

I won't let that happen again. I'll act and not choke, Holden promised himself, weaving the three of them through the maze of boxes and pallets, of shrink-wrapped loads of items they had no idea existed until they had the keys to the kingdom in their possession.

Then Will's stomach grumbled in the silence.

"Holden, do you think we can find some food and rest for a second?" Holden nodded and made their way to the access stairway to the first floor that security only took. He pressed the card against the activator on the stairwell wall, watching it light up green. He turned the handle, waiting to hear something or see movement within the stairwell. Once he panned around with the flashlight and got no response, they moved inside and went downstairs.

The food court stockrooms were amazing. They were stocked so well that it would be years before they would need to resupply. Apparently, the mall was well-prepared for Christmas rush and then some.

The day after Christmas; the biggest return day of the year. Holden was almost positive that's what the overstock was for.

Immediately, Holden and the others could smell the cooked food from the other side of the security doors. It made them hungry just thinking about how much food was available on the other side of the door. Will snuck a peek through the security door port window, looking from section to section for movement. When he found none, he looked to the other two.

"Do you think it's safe to go out?"

Holden looked out as well for a moment, panning his eyes around the area. He wasn't used to seeing it this quiet in the mall. Even during opening and closing hours before customers came in, there was at least a movement of janitors and workers moving stock from one place to another. Even the mall decorators and Santa and his elves had been in early and stayed late for the holiday rush.

Holden motioned to Melissa to see if she wanted to take a look. She shook her head and backed away.

"No, thanks. I like it fine right here where I'm at."

Holden nodded and turned off his flashlight. He moved them all closer to him, speaking in a hushed tone.

"I think one of us should go and get food for all of us. That way, we can keep the door locked and secure and another can be look out. This is a thick door. They can't get through a metal door like this. Volunteers, anyone?"

Will looked like he was going to be sick but he

raised his hand anyway.

"I'll go." Holden handed him the flashlight, hooking the keys to his own belt loop.

They had decided on *Hunan Kitchen*, a local Chinese Food eatery that they frequented during their lunch breaks. Holden swiped his access card and opened the door to the food court just enough so Will could slide through, shutting it back as soon as Will was out.

Will didn't need to use the flashlight for light; the main lights were still on as well as the festive ones, blinking decorative lights as well as white-lit wreaths hung on corners of the food court walls, Will's eyes scanning each table, chair and trash area for anything out of the ordinary. He gripped the Maglite tightly in his hand and prepared a wild swing for whatever he encountered.

*　　　　　*　　　　　*

Holden and Melissa watched as Will disappeared down the back corridor between the eateries, out of sight until he made it back or shouted a warning.

Holden leaned against the wall, looking around at all of the unopened boxes around them, when Melissa spoke.

"It's yes."

Holden lifted his head up, looking at her.

"What's yes?"

"Will I go out with you, you know, to the movies? The answer is yes."

Holden blushed. He could feel the lump in his throat begin again, this time for a different reason than before. He was sad that all this had happened. It had stomped on his possible life at other things. *And here, all I was trying to do was have a normal life. Blood thirsty creatures from the dark and a Zombie Santa kept that from happening, alright!*

There was nothing he could say. She said yes and that's all he needed.

But with the moment, with the circumstance, with the death all around them, Holden didn't hesitate any longer. He grabbed for her and pulled her close, feeling her snake bite piercings press against his mouth and not caring one bit. He kissed her and let all of his desire out with the kiss, feeling her arms wrap themselves around him, his own arms cradling her in the process.

They let themselves need the other.

*   *   *

Will didn't have to get out into the open food court area. There was a small hallway that attached all of the eateries to one another, allowing for free movement in the stock areas and to the restrooms without having to go out through the food court itself, which Will used now as he traversed to Hunan Kitchen. It took no time at all as he held the swinging door open just enough so he could slip in and out.

He grabbed three Styrofoam to-go trays and a large serving spoon, dumping helping after helping into the trays until they were bulging full, closing one after another until he had three completely full trays next to him. He looked around for something to carry them in and found a soy sauce box half full of sauce packets, setting them down inside of it.

He grabbed a handful of silverware, a few sodas from the packed ice they sat in and a handful of napkins and was out of there before he could say Kung—Pao chicken, moving silently back through the double doors and to a half-opened security door with his friends on the other side. They locked it back and made their way further into the bowels of the mall.

*   *   *

"So, what do you think they are, anyway; these things?" Will dropped the last bite of his chicken teriyaki back onto the tray it came from, unable to eat it. The two others looked stuffed, too, Melissa lying on a cot while Holden leaned against her.

It had been a few hours since the three of them had left the food court. They had found a security guard office with a locker room, shower stalls, a few elliptical and treadmill machines, and a room with some pretty comfy cots, which they used now, the empty trays of *Hunan Kitchen* littering the floor.

The three of them moved the cots closer together, forming an odd-shaped triangle, still speaking softly.

Earlier, while they were eating, they heard movement: scuffles, shouts and some eruption of violence broke out in another part of the mall, but they were so far away they didn't know what part it could be coming from. They were just glad it wasn't on their side of the security doors.

Holden felt Melissa's fingers running through his hair, closing his eyes in thought.

"I think they're people. I mean Santa Claus was a person. It was Cornelius, the old man we made the lattes for all those times. He was just a regular old man; but looking at him when the craziness started, he no longer looked like himself."

Melissa shot out her theory.

"The way that everyone got it, it looks like it's based on a virus. I mean, they seemed to transfer it from one person to the next until everyone was one of them."

Will pulled the cot blanket up over his

shoulders, sitting up a little bit from the cot, propping himself up on one elbow.

"So, if that's the case, then Wan is one now, too, huh?"

Holden just nodded. "I bet he is. He got bit by one of them."

Melissa just shook her head. "Man, I need a cigarette!" Holden slipped a pack from his pocket stealthily, pulling out a lighter with it as well.

"You're a lifesaver, sweetie!" Melissa took the pack from him and grabbed the lighter, about to light up. Holden pointed up to the ceiling, motioning to the smoke alarms and the sprinkler systems.

"I think the showers are the only safe place to smoke around here, unless we go back out to the roof."

Melissa got up from her cot and threw the blanket aside, taking the cigarettes and lighter out with her. Holden motioned to Will as he got up as well.

"Wanna come have a smoke with us, Will?"

Will just shook his head and laid back on his cot, covering his arms over his eyes.

"Naw, dawg. It's all you. I'm just gonna get some rest for a minute."

Holden followed Melissa back to the showers, flashlight in hand. She sat on a bench at the end of the stalls, a stack of towels on a shelf up above her. Holden watched her for a moment as she took out a cigarette and lit it in the dim corner, leaving the lights off in the shower stalls.

It was night outside anyway. Time for things to go to sleep. I wonder if those things out there, The Dead, even sleep.

He sat next to her and took a smoke off of hers, leaning his head against the cold stone walls behind them. She took a drag off the cigarette.

"What do we do now, Holden? Is the entire world like this? Is it just in Bloomington? Can we even kill them?"

Holden didn't know what to say to all those questions. All he knew is that he felt safe for the moment, whereas he hadn't hours earlier, running for his life.

He didn't know what his next step was. His mind hadn't let him get that far. But he knew that he would never take things for granted again.

Even the little things, Holden thought. *Movies, time with Angela and Marcus as part of his Big Brother program at the group home, sitting with friends and talking.*

And that kiss. His mind swam when he thought about it, but he allowed his thoughts to get caught up with the fantasy of it. He had never exactly had a normal home life, but he at least had a chance to get to know what normal felt like. Melissa finished her cigarette and dropped it on the stone floor, putting it out with the heel of her shoe. She stood up.

"I do know something though, Holden."

He looked up at her as she stood in front of him.

"What's that?" He took another cigarette out of the pack and grabbed for the lighter that was sitting on the bench next to him.

"I'm about to use one of those showers and get clean." She grabbed a towel from the shelf above him, unbuckling her work belt from around her waist. She slipped her shoes off and tossed them to the side, pulling down her work slacks so that only her long shirt hung down, Holden getting a glimpse of her panties before she planted a kiss on him.

"Care to join me, Employee of the month?"

15

It was the end of the world and all was fine in Holden's world. In the showers, he found out what it was like to let go. Holden and Melissa held each other for the longest time, terrified to let go of one another, scared that the world would fall apart even more. Once they were naked and under the steaming hot water, their tears at the losses around them flowed like a wellspring, Holden cradling Melissa in his arms until the weeping stopped.

They were not dead, that enough was true.

He kissed her and she kissed him back. She felt good to touch, her skin felt good to taste, her moans increased at the same time the kisses down her body did, the young man hungry for her. He grabbed her naked ass in his hands and pulled her close, kissing her on the lips. She wrapped her arms around his neck and let her be taken in by the intensity of it all.

Melissa could feel Holden's erection harden between his legs, pressing against her soft skin, her nipples hardening against his chest from his touch. She urged him for more, pressing herself against the back wall of the shower, pulling him to her. Holden felt Melissa's fingers wrap around his erection and lead him inside her.

They moaned in unison.

"Don't stop, Holden! Please don't stop!" They tore at each other, pressing and pulling, biting and sucking, every thrust each of them made a signal for more from the other. Holden held onto the shower head as he pressed into her, his other hand guiding her hips against him.

She cried out to him, grabbing at his waist as she led him further inside her.

"Don't stop, Holden! Don't stop!"

And Holden listened well. They did not stop until the water grew cold and their bodies were shaking from pleasure, both of them pressed against each other for warmth.

Apart, they were cold and alone. But, together, they were warm and wanted by the other. They held each other until the pleasure subsided.

*   *   *

Weeks passed by for Angela and Marcus. It was Christmas Eve and all was silent.

They are hand in hand, dancing together. The lights are off to keep The Dead away and the music is turned down to a whisper. But it doesn't stop The Dead from coming through the barricaded door.

Marcus drops the table leg and watches as The Dead convulses a moment longer and then falls limp and goes still for good, a puddle of blood pooling underneath where he had struck it.

"Oh my god, Marcus! When will they stop coming?"

"I don't know, Angela! That's the third one that's come from inside the house in the last few hours. I've looked everywhere but I can't find out how they got in the building! I blocked all the exits weeks ago." Angela's eyes widened with surprise.

"Maybe they came from the basement of the building. You haven't checked there since when we first got here."

"And I don't plan on it, either. We don't have any way of looking around down there." Marcus held up the dead flashlight.

"And the batteries in our flashlight have been dead for days. There's no way I'm going down there without a light and leave you here!"

Marcus moves towards the zombie but Angela just holds onto him even tighter.

"Where are you going, Marcus?" Marcus can hear the fear in her voice, this time more than ever.

She's losing it even more. My baby is losing it right in front of me and I can't do anything about it! But Marcus did his best to comfort her before he moved any further away.

"Honey, I'm just going to get rid of the body. I can't just leave it sitting there!"

"Just leave it, Marcus! There's no point in moving it because there's no place to put it. We can't open the doors, the windows.... Anything." She looked around at the place that they were supposed to be starting their new lives in. It was unrecognizable from what it had been, and that was only a few weeks ago. "We're trapped inside of our own house!"

"I remember a time when you didn't mind being trapped in here with me at all. I actually remember you calling in to work to stay with me. Remember that?"

Angela nodded and, for a second, a smile moves across her face. She looks around at their home and how it has been demolished in just a short amount of time just for the purpose of survival.

As Marcus moves the still form of The Dead across the floor, it smears blood and chunks of brain and bone in a zigzag fashion.

Angela nearly gags in response to the smell.

"Uuuggghh! How disgusting! I still can't get used to the smell of them, Marcus."

"I don't think you're supposed to be getting used to it. It's going to be okay though."

"The Dead are coming through our walls trying

to kill us, Marcus! This isn't exactly the ideal of living conditions, you know! I would think you'd be more supportive!" Angela begins crying into her arms.

There is movement outside the main entry door.

"Shhhhhhh! Baby, they'll hear us! Remember, that's how they came for us in the first place."

"I'm sorry, Marcus. I know, I know. I just don't know how to feel anymore. I try, baby, I try, don't I?"

"Yes, you try. That's what counts the most."

"An A for effort, huh?" She wipes her tears away with her hand.

"An A-plus, baby. An A-plus."

Suddenly, there is a wailing going on outside their door and the barricade planks splinter even further and the door starts to lean open again, revealing a number of Dead just outside. Both Marcus and Angela stand up and run over to the door, leaning their backs against the door to hold it steady.

Angela whispered. "Oh, no, Marcus! Not again!" The pain and the anguish in her face was almost too much for Marcus to bear. Angela closes her eyes and winces every time their door rattles. She tries her best but Marcus watches and she begins to break apart again, from the inside out.

"Just hold on and stay quiet. Just like last time."

The moans are louder this time and there is a beating on the door. The beating is light at first but then there are more footfalls in the hallway and, just outside, more of the Dead begin pounding on the door.

Angela is about to scream when Marcus puts his hand over her mouth, letting her hold her hands over her ears. That stops her from screaming but she moves away from him shortly and to another part of the room.

Marcus's eyes grow wide with fear. "Baby, I

can't hold this by myself! You have to help me!
Baby! Baby?"

But Angela isn't listening. She sits down on the
floor and covers her ears, talking to herself.

"It was better before.   It was better before.
Things were simpler then. It was so much better
before this."

*   *   *

The ornaments were always her favorite things.
They were so many colors, bright reds and greens,
silvers and golds, shimmering and shining on the
tree like a beacon of happiness. Angela looks
down and notices that she's finished with another
box of her favorite ornaments. She moves the
empty box from atop the full one and begins
placing the new box of ornaments onto the tree.

Marcus finishes with the thin icicles on one side
of the tree and moves over to her side. She looks

over at him, smiling.

"You'll never guess what I got you for Christmas."

"I hope it's not a pair of socks or underwear. I think Mom and Dad got those covered this year."

"Quit being silly and let's finish this tree!"

Angela hands Marcus an ornament from the box below.

Marcus continues the conversation. "What about you? Aren't you interested in knowing what I got you?"

"How do you known I don't already know what you got me?"

"Oh, really?"

"Really."

Marcus puts the ornament on the tree and begins to sneak slyly over to Angela, Angela giggling girlishly.

"Then I guess I'm going to have to torture you until I find out the information I need, huh?"

Marcus begins tickling her and she tries to push him away but he's too strong. His arms enfold around her and she feels safe for the moment. Marcus pulls her in for a kiss.

"We're never going to get this tree finished with a troublemaker like you around."

Angela finally breaks the hold he has on her after the kiss and sits down on the floor, digging through the rest of the boxes for more of her favorite ornaments.

"Marcus?"

"Yes, baby." He is busy finishing up the icicles on her side of the tree.

"There's something I have to tell you."

*   *   *

"Angela! Angela, listen to me!"

Angela comes back to her senses, looking at the terror-filled face of her fiancée as he tries to reach her.

"Help me or we'll be their food!"

Suddenly, two dead hands break past the splintered wood behind the door barricade and reach for Marcus. Angela screams and Marcus tries to find something to cover the holes in the door.

"Angela, help me!"

Angela holds the barricaded door until Marcus can find something else in the room to fix it with. He grabs the last of the cabinet doors that are stacked by the kitchen entrance and begins hammering them into place once he pushes the hands of the Dead away, bringing more muffled voices outside the door with the noise. The banging grows louder and louder outside.

"What are we going to do, Marcus?"

Marcus speaks to her as softly as possible without raising more noise on their side. "We just have to wait it out."

*   *   *

The crowd around the fire barrel were quiet for a time once Scout stopped his story, letting them all take in what he had told them.

Derrick was the first one to speak. His response wasn't so positive. "So they die? That's how you end the story, with the only people that survived through the beginning getting eaten alive by The Dead? Man, you really suck at storytelling, Scout!"

"How was that a love story, Scout? That shit was depressing as fuck," Derrick chided in, throwing another log on the fire in front of them, rubbing his hands together for further warmth.

Scout eyed the rest of the crew of the BRB, taking in each of their facial expressions now, the shocked looks plastered on each of their faces proof that the story did its job. Gordon's face even carried that look, though he was nowhere near as shocked as the others because he at least knew a little bit of Scout's background.

He knows my real name, that's all that matters here, Scout concluded, warming his own hands by the fire, letting the silence from the end of the story spill across the rest of the crew.

"But it's not real, right? Everyone died in the first wave of The Dead. It's just a story." Derrick looked around at the faces of the others, waiting for someone to speak up, for someone to comfort the uneasiness that was beginning to fill in the spaces of the silence around them.

Gordon motioned to Scout then with a quick nod of the head.

"Tell them, Scout. Finish what you started."

The crew looked over at Gordon then, amazed that he didn't seem as in the dark with the information that had been given as they presently were.

Scout unzipped his thick jacket and pulled out a

creased, beat up composition book that he had kept hidden close to his chest. He held it out for every one of the crew to see.

"This is the journal of Marcus Green. I found it when I went looking for him."

All of the crew's eyes gazed in awe that the story had just come to life more than it ever could have. Derrick was skeptical immediately.

"When you went looking for him? How did you know him, Scout? I thought this was just a story like all the others we've told, just something to pass the time." That's when the answer came spilling out of Scout. From the very deepest spot within his heart, the truth came tumbling out.

"Because my real name is Holden McCall and this is my story."

Scout didn't look anything like the young Holden McCall he had told of in the last few hours, that's true. But with what had transpired all those years ago and what is still happening all around them, no one looked the same from the day The Dead became the majority and the living the minority.

From the months foraging on his own with his friend and hiding out in a warehouse until they could formulate a plan of escape back into the real world, Holden had changed.   He had also changed when meeting the camp in such dire circumstances, covered in his friend's blood and begging for help.

He had known what it would cost him; his life.

Now was just Holden's way of surviving the world around him. The tears on his face had run into his beard and he did little to stop them, only wiping at his runny nose with his gloved hand.

"I'll read to you the last entry, then you'll know what happened to Marcus and Angela."

Holden leaned the book down so the light from the fire reflected onto its worn and tattered pages, looking down at the words and clearing his throat before speaking.

"'They've come for us now. They know we're hiding from them and there's nothing we can do...'"

16

And wait it out they did.

Hours go by and the muffled murmurs soon slip away, one by one, until there are only two or three constant moans on the other side of the door, allowing Marcus and Angela some time to rest. Both of them are covered in sweat from holding the wooden panels in place and they collapse down on the floor next to each other once the door can finally fend for itself with the little numbers behind it.

"See, I think they're gone now." There's a smile

on Marcus' face, a small victory taken from this moment. Angela slides herself down onto the cold floor, letting the exhaustion take her over. Marcus moves over to the refrigerator in the kitchen and brings back a bottle of water for them both. His fiancée takes it eagerly and drinks most of the contents of the bottle in a few gulps. She tries her best to give Marcus a smile back.

"I thought that was the end for a moment there."

Marcus takes a drink from his own water, wiping his mouth with the sleeve of his shirt.

"Honey, don't say those kinds of things. As long as we keep this place secure, we'll be okay."

Marcus looks at Angela then. He still sees the sadness in her eyes. He's concerned for her more than he's ever been before. He climbs back around her and slips his arm around her waist, cradling her head with his other arm.

"Honey, you look exhausted. Let me hold you

for a while. Get some sleep. I'll get some more wood to board up the door later. It looks like they've all gone for at least a little while."

He holds her close, feeling her heartbeat through his own body, her skin so close, her breathing so ragged and labored.

She's doing her best to hold it together in a time like this, Marcus noticed, watching her.

"I want you to open your present now, Marcus." Angela sits up from the floor, moving over towards the dimly lit tree.

"Baby, it's not even Christmas yet!"

"I don't want to wait until then."

"Oh, okay. If it can't wait."

"It can't, Marcus."

Angela walks over to the Christmas Tree, getting Marcus' gift from under the tree. She walks back over to him and hands it to him.

"Open it."

Marcus looks at her then at the gift and slowly

begins to open it. It's a small box, almost the size of a jewelry box and, when he opens it, there's a small piece of folded up paper in it. He unfolds the paper and looks at it for a long time.

"Baby, is this what I think it is?"

Angela leans a bit closer and looks at the paper with him. She smiles as she gives him further details.

"Yes, it is. There, that's the legs, those are the arms, and, well, that's the rest of your son."

"Baby, are you serious? We're going to have a boy?"

Angela nods her head happily and Marcus grabs her up, spinning her around.

"That's great, baby! That's wonderful news!"

From a distance away, a breaking noise can be heard. Glass breaks into several hundred pieces and more moaning sounds can be heard, now from another direction other than the front door.

Marcus moves quickly to where his table leg

had been left, picking it up to prepare for a possible confrontation. He slips the piece of paper into his pocket and drops the empty package onto the floor.

"They've found another way in!"

"What are we going to do?"

"I don't know! I don't know what else we can do!" Angela moves closer to Marcus, curling under his arm for protection, even if it is only momentary.

"Hold me!" And Marcus does just that, listening to the rattling of the wood beams as they come loose on the front door, listening to the moans of The Dead as they push their way in the rest of the way.

There was nothing that they could do. They could hide on the balcony until they were found out and then were overtaken, but they might be out there for days in the cold weather, killing their own selves in the process.

Marcus grabs hold of Angela tighter and pulls

his sobbing fiancée hard against his chest, both holding each other in what they know will be their last embrace.

The wood splinters and Marcus and Angela hear them scurry through the crack in the door, moving towards them. They only have moments left.

"Here they come!" He grabs Angela by the face and kisses her hard. "I love you, baby."

Angela lets the tears pour down her face, knowing the end is near. She kisses him back, just as hard, biting his lip as he pulls away. He places his hand to her belly and looks at her, tears in his own eyes.

*　　　　*　　　　*

The three Yum-E-Buns employees had been in hiding for two weeks since the mall massacre happened all those days ago. They slept most of the time, keeping as still as possible in the mall back inventory rooms, making sure they weren't heard until the last of The Dead were gone.

No military came. No ambulances or fire trucks blared their sirens through the streets. It was not mass chaos as the movies and t.v. shows made it to be; we did not go out with a fight. We went out in a state of panic and with a fizzle.

Now there was just quiet; a deathly quiet that surrounded the city of Bloomington, Illinois that holiday season, complete with the silent nights and snowy mornings.

The three of them decided to venture out and find out if there were any other survivors in the city. They had checked their phones and social media had gone on full blast with videos of others encountering The Dead as well as finding places to hide such as they did. But, even on social media, it was still difficult to locate their families and friends, hoping beyond hope that many had just lost their phones amid the chaos.

And there was no word from Marcus or Angela. There had been no posts or updates from them, almost as if they had stopped existing. Holden needed to find a way to their new place. After Marcus got the new job, they had moved into the condos not far from the mall; *Bloomington Estates, they were called*. Holden had even helped them move in.

With backpacks they had found in the summer inventory from the sporting goods store and a few baseball bats and golf clubs, the three Yum-E-Buns employees armed themselves with weapons and new attire and walked out onto the second level of the Stratford Square Mall.

Nothing was the same was the first thought that went through their minds. The lights had remained on in the building, but the festive atmosphere had been changed more into a tomb for the masses that were dead all around.

"Almost no one made it out." Melissa tightened her grip on the nine iron in her hand, stepping over pieces of body parts everywhere. By now, the blood had dried on the floors and it was sticky as they walked on mall floors, which were usually well-shined and sparkling.

Will pointed his golf club to the bloody footsteps that scattered throughout different parts of the mall.

"And, if they did make it out, it wasn't as a person. Look at those strides, it's like they're leaping from spot to spot."

"Quiet, guys." Holden lifted the bat to his lips, carefully walking over the floor full of cadavers until they had made it to the escalator. But the escalator was jam-packed with bodies, too, making it impossible to walk down.

"They tried to escape and died on the escalator." The horrified faces were frozen in their death scream, dozens of chewed up bodies piled atop one another on both escalator, the escalators long having since worked once the pieces of body parts had started clogging up the motors.

Will pointed over at the stairway just a few shops over with his golf club, walking back out and around the remains with the other two. They all covered their noses with their shirts as they moved further and further into the mall, the smell intensifying.

"We can go down through there. It looks clear enough."

They moved back around the remains and walked over to the stairway. Will was the first one to make it over there. What he saw made him stop short.

"No, there's bodies here as well." He looked down the stairwell and saw a number of bodies piled atop one another. It wasn't until he turned back around to backtrack that they started moving, unlocking themselves from one another until the Dead now outnumbered the living. There were eight Dead that sprung after the three of them.

Will forgot his quiet backtracking methods and took a swing at the first one with his golf club, smashing its head open with the first swing.

"Get out of here! Back to the door!"

Melissa and Holden turned back and ran through the bloody remains as quick as they could, slipping, stumbling at times on the scattered pieces of limbs that had been strewn across the mall floors. The Dead gained on them in moments. Holden turned to defend himself.

As he swung, he could feel the adrenaline to stay alive pumping through his body, almost instantaneous upon the first swing. He batted one down quick and slammed the edge of his bat into its skull, swinging upward to stop another in its tracks moving straight towards him.

All this time, but they never faltered in their attacks, never showed fear of death or doubted their actions. They were free of consequences and risked it all every time.

Death was such a curious thing to Holden. He never understood it, he had never felt it before. It had never reached its stench-coated hand out to him and offered eternity to him before. As he swung at the third Dead that approached, he did not fear for his life. He was ready to die. He was happy taking down as many of these that he could.

He took down the third, then another, beating and crushing their skulls open on the already bloodied floor as he did so, preparing himself for the next one that came at him.

But Death doesn't take you when you're ready, when you've manned up and accepted your fate.

It takes you when you're not ready, when you're beat down. Or it takes you when you're happy with things and least expecting it.

When Death reached its hand over to Melissa that day and grabbed her up by the throat, tearing her into pieces before her lover, a piece inside of Holden died that day. No number of swings could save her. He could beat the Dead as they lined up before him, letting his arms do the work, switching to his body, spinning from one side to the next until he had given his arms a proper rest.

But the look of fear that he saw in Melissa's eyes as one got past him and moved through his swing, he couldn't stop that one. And neither could she. She swung wide and left, trying to move away from it as it pounced upon her, its fingers and teeth going wild.

"Nooooooo!" Holden drove the end of his bat through a nearby creature's chest, ripping it out to approach the one on Melissa. But it had already started its dance of death upon her flesh.

She screamed for Holden to help her, her nervous fingers dropping her golf club in the process.

"Help me, Holden!" She reached out for him. The Dead tore her apart right before his eyes. By the time he had made it to her, it had already torn a gash into her neck, feeding on her blood. It tore thick swathes into her chest and face as it fed, forgetting all others of her party.

She gurgled in an attempt to breathe, dropping to her knees, her feet slipping on her own blood that pumped out of her in spurts all over her new clothes.

Holden swung the bat so hard it broke across the creature's head, splintering the wood in two. A piece of the bat went flying out over the balcony, the young man using the leftover piece to drive it into the Dead's shattered skull.

It folded in on itself and fell over, Holden tossing

it to one side. He grabbed for Melissa and pulled her closer, looking around to see if there were any more coming their way. It was clear at the moment. Will had finished his last Dead off and moved closer to see Melissa on the ground. Tears filled like wells at the corner of Holden's eyes.

"No, no, no, no! Not Melissa! Please, not her!"

Melissa grabbed Holden's hand tightly, squeezing it as hard as she could. She stared up at him with those longing eyes, twinges of pain erupting in them from moment to moment.

"I love you, Holden McCall."

Holden pulled her closer, kissing her softly on the forehead.

"I love you, too, Melissa!"

She grabbed her nine iron up from the floor where it had fallen in her own blood. Tears welled up in her eyes as her body shook slightly.

Holden wiped the tears that fell from his eyes with his shoulder, watching as she pushed the golf club into his bloodied hand.

"I would have gone to every movie with you." She coughed and began to spasm, her eyes drifting away for a moment, then coming back to him.

"Do it, Holden. Don't let me be them." She turned her head to the Dead around them. She pushed him away from her with the last of the strength she had.

Holden stood up and looked over at Will, his friend and co-worker sobbing openly now. He shook his head.

Holden looked down at Melissa again. She smiled at him. Her body had calmed its shaking. Her eyes were beginning to get a glossy tint to them.

She spoke to him one last time. It was barely a whisper.

"Do it, Holden. Do it for us. Do it for the memory of us."

Holden raised the golf club above his head, tears streaming down his face. His whole body shook with pain. His vision blurred.

He struck down as hard as he could.

Epilogue

Scout and the others packed up the rest of the supplies into the underbelly of the BRB and closed the container doors, checking the undercarriage of the beast of a vehicle before climbing in. Scout moved to climb back up onto the roof when Gordon stopped him, grabbing his shoulder.

"You already took the last shift. You need to get some rest before we go in. You might need it."

But the look on Scout's face showed Gordon that there was no arguing with him.

"I got us here.   I want to bring us in the rest of the way."

"Are you okay after all that?" Gordon motioned to the fire barrel that one of his men was putting out, tossing snow into the barrel by the handfuls.

"I'm fine." Scout's eyes looked up at the BRB then back at Gordon.

"Everyone has a story. I'm sure you have a story about this bus, right? You didn't just acquire it out of the blue, you didn't just survive by being you. You had to find something-"

"-that kept me alive during the hard times. I got it, you're good now. That's all fine and good. But, if no one told you, I'm sorry for your loss, Holden."

Scout smiled at his real name, adjusting the

rifle on his shoulder, reaching inside his winter coat for something. He pulled out a small plastic baggie with something in it, handing it to Gordon.

"That's if they decide to doubt the story. And it's for you. That's who we're looking for."

It was the I.D. badge of Dr. Collin Moore.

"If the research facility is still there, maybe this will get us in so we can see how to cure this thing." Scout grabbed at one of the rungs of the ladder that led up to the roof of the vehicle.

"Wait a second, Holden." Gordon slipped the baggie with the doctor's badge into his coat pocket, zipping it up.

"What you said back there, all of it. Why did you call it A Christmas Love Story?"

Scout hesitated for a moment. His eyes welled up with tears then, letting them flow again now that everyone else was packed in the bus.

"I went back there, Gordon, to where Angela

and Marcus had barricaded themselves. And they died together. At least, from what I found that was left of them. It was such a mess. And I found a gift for me under their tree. And do you know what it was, Gordon?"

Gordon shook his head, captivated by the young man's story.

"It was Marcus' journal and the badge. He wrote a note in the book and it said, 'I hope this gift finds you alive and well. And, if it does, that means there's a chance to make things right.'"

"He gave me a fighting chance, Gordon. And that's all I can do now; fight at your side and have hope that there's a chance."

Gordon patted Holden on the shoulder. Seeing so much hurt in the young man's eyes nearly tore the older man apart. The two of them heard someone start the BRB and the metal beast rumbled to life.

"Now, can we please drive this monster into

the city and get this over with?" Holden wiped his eyes and grabbed the bottom rung of the ladder to pull himself up with.

"You got it." Gordon lifted himself up into the vehicle and pressed the hydraulic doors shut behind him, signaling to Scout with a quick flashing of the lights. In another moment, the BRB pulled back out onto the main road, Scout atop his perch, grabbing for his holds to keep himself steady.

He made sure the rifle wasn't frozen by loading and unloading it again, picking the shells up off the top of the cabin. He wiped the off the snow that had gotten on the shells and reloaded them.

Scout slung the rifle up and over his head, hanging it on his shoulder. He felt for the belay hooks on the roof of the BRB and wiped the snow away, connecting them the harness at his waist without looking, the act long having since become second nature to him.

He looked out over the city of Bloomington, a sadness in his eyes. The snow came down now, as hard as it had all those years ago when he first escaped this place. All of the lights were out, including the blinking one on the water tower not far away from the entrance to the city. The place looked like a dry husk of its former self, a barren wasteland compared to the frenzy of activity that had frequented it. Scout would be surprised if they found even one survivor on their trip through it.

But I'm a survivor of this place, the young man decided, so many years already on his back, so much his eyes had already seen that he could never unsee. And, with that thought, he welcomed the unknown within Bloomington and hoped that the human race did indeed have a chance to take back what they had lost; their humanity.

Not even close
to the end...

- Afterword -

By Titus Strong

I don't even know where to start with this.
Ah, first things first! It all started back in 2006 in
Baltimore, Maryland. I was teaching Drama I, II,
and III that first semester and there was a play
writing contest at Drexel University in
Philadelphia, PA. I wanted my students to enter
so I wrote them a sample over Thanksgiving
Break.

The responses I got during the Cold Reading
in class were insane! They wanted to perform it
and, in another few weeks, we got approval and
A Christmas Love Story was performed before
Christmas Break. Of course, it was nothing like

the novel is; only a fraction of the scenes were used and it was only about Marcus and Angela in the play and all the other actors were zombie extras.

But, in those 10 years in between then and now, the melting pot in my head began stirring. And, after writing a few erotic fiction novels, I found that my voice could possibly speak in another genre that I had not tried before; a horror novel. And not just any horror novel but a zombie horror novel! Oh, fuck yes! I had always had my own version of zombies that I thought were scary, taking some of the strongest parts from classic zombies and merging them into what you see within these pages.

Yes, this is only the beginning, ladies and gentlemen.

OTHER BOOKS BY WUNDERLANND PRESS PUBLISHING

A Man's Romance Novel:

- **The Temptress: Book One (August 2011)**
- A Corporate Feeling: Book Two (Summer 2017)
- Teach Me: Book Three
- Domesticating the Inner Hound: Book Four

Festive Tales of Erotic Fiction: Short Story Collections

- **How Santa Ate My Cookies and Other Festive Tales of Erotic Fiction: Christmas Special (Nov 2016)**

A Young Gentleman's Romance Novel:

- **The Pill: (Released October 2014)**
- The Pill: Second Dose (TBA)
- The Pill: Possible Solutions (TBA)

The Realm of Sound Novels:

- **Demi's Flute: Book One (Released March 2015)**

A Zombie Survival School Prelude Series Novels:

- **A Christmas Love Story: (October 2016)**
- Surplus (TBA)
- brb (TBA)
- The Prom (TBA)

A Zombie Survival School Novel Series:

- Monster Machinations: Book One (TBA)

The Chronicles of Ar Solon Series:

- Book 10: The Elixir (TBA)
- Book 11: Day of the Ever-Wanderers (TBA)
- Book 17: In the Care of Kobolds (TBA)
- Book 18: Chains of Solace (TBA)
- **Book 19: Forgotten Angel (April 2010)**
- Book 20: The Paths We All Walk: A Collection of Tales (TBA)
- **Book 21: The Healer, Part I (August 2011)**
- **Book 21: The Healer, Part II (Dec 2016)**
- Book 22: Plague of the Elves (TBA)

The Wunderlannd Novel Series:

- **Edward in Wunderlannd (Oct 2011)**
- **Edward and The Enfeebled (Dec. 2012)**

- The Further, further, and Much More Further Adventures of Edward Krimp (Dec 2016)
- The Annotated Edward: A Comprehensive, In-depth look at the Edward trilogy (TBA)

Non-fiction:

Traveling Triumphs: From Budapest and Beyond (Released May 2013)

About the Author

Little is known about **Titus Strong** and he likes it that way. He's traveled a bit, written a bit, lived life enough for three regular men. He has worked close with Wunderlannd Press for years, publishing The Temptress with them in 2011. He had three novel series now: *A Man's Romance Novel, A*

Young Gentleman's Romance Novel, and *The Zombie Survival School Novel series*, which the first book, *A Christmas Love Story*, is being adapted as a graphic novel. He is presently writing sequels to The Temptress and The Pill for release in 2017. Titus presently lives in a state of euphoria and enjoys his nightly escapades with great privacy.

About the Cover Artist

PRESTON RISHAW was born and raised in the Poconos and has lived in Middle Tennessee for the last 30 years. He has been the chief preparator for MTSU's Department of Art for the last 25 years, and a chief library advisor for Linebaugh Public Library for the last 20 years. He is also a freelance illustrator, collaborating with Wunderlannd Press Publishing since 2015. Preston is presently working on the graphic novel adaptation to *A Christmas Love Story* and has completed the cover for *The Annotated Edward*, a detailed collection of the first three Wunderlannd Novels in the series. He is husband to Tina, father to Loretta, and cares for his mother Patricia.

Now you can order your
Exclusive Books and Merchandise from
Wunderlannd Press Publishing directly!

GO TO: mkt.com/wunderlanndpress **or** use the QR
Code below with your tablet or mobile device for great
goodies only available on the company store. You can
even get limited copies autographed and personalized by
select authors free of charge.

Also available for purchase at these local retailer sites:
www.amazon.com and www.bandn.com,
www.alibris.com